UNFOLDING

Other books by Jonathan Friesen

Aquifer

Both of Me

Middle-grade novels

The Last Martin

Aldo's Fantastical Movie Palace

UNFOLDING

A NOVEL

JONATHAN FRIESEN

BLINK

BLINK

Unfolding
Copyright © 2017 by Jonathan Friesen

This title is also available as a Blink ebook.

Requests for information should be addressed to:
Blink, 3900 Sparks Drive SE, Grand Rapids, Michigan 49546

ISBN 978-0-310-74833-5

Cover design: Ron Huizinga
Interior design: Denise Froehlich

Printed in the United States of America

17 18 19 20 21 22 /DHV/ 20 19 18 17 16 15 14 13 12 11 10 9 8 7 6 5 4 3 2 1

She dropped from the Oklahoma sky.

A gift. Proof of the Almighty's existence.

But the Miracle Baby could not have descended with less fanfare. The citizens of Gullary, huddled in bathtubs and hidden in shelters, missed her arrival. Their collective heads were face-to-floor as seven tornadoes danced through the night.

The tornadoes traveled over five hundred miles. They teased and jabbed their twisty fingers toward the earth, only to rear back and punch through the green with a fury rarely seen previous, and only once since. And on one such strike, heaven—or hell, depending which side you're on—opened its fist and gently stole a child before pulling back up into the angry sky.

How far the swirling clouds carried the child is anyone's guess. But that she was set down with the care of a new mother is a *fact*, one my parents emerged to when the wind paused and the rain fell straight. She was wide-eyed and peaceful, still in her cradle, calm beneath soaked pink swaddling.

Ma found her first. Ms. Pickering, our neighbor, was a close second, though this detail contains some wriggle room. She joined Ma in leaning over the baby girl, and in the moment of that child's deepest distress . . .

"Martha Pickering, get on inside and see to your own!" Ma muscled Ms. P out of the way. "I'm caring for this babe."

"No. The rights to her are mine. She landed on my property." Ms. P paused and looked to heaven and whispered, "He has seen my sadness and sent me a replacement child."

As was customary, their argument raged until Dad intervened. He eyeballed the cradle. Our neighbor had a point: Everything but the child's feet rested on Ms. P's unmown front yard.

"Come on, more storms are comin'," Dad said, tugging on Ma's arm. "Martha says she's gonna deal with her properly. There's no denying where she landed."

Ma pursed her lips and swiped wet from her brow. Her gray-tinged hair, normally kept on the straight and narrow, swept wild and matted across her face. I envision her here an overweight John the Baptist, straight from the wilderness. "Well now, I suppose, as Solomon is not present to solve this dilemma." She rose and stomped toward our trailer home while Ms. Pickering gently carried the baby next door.

I've often wondered how life would have been different had God's finger nudged that cradle six inches eastward, had Ma carried the little one into our home, where I lay two months old and sleeping in the bathtub. Would she have shared a tub with me, Jonah Everett III, her first night in town?

Turns out the girl landed along with a dowry. Morning revealed a living cow and a grandfather clock also settled on the Pickerings' lawn, cementing Ms. P's claim on the baby's care.

News of the miracle traveled quickly. Hordes of reporters recast our town as more than the hardened home of a Supermax prison. A columnist from *The Oklahoman* penned it best:

Here in Gullary, Oklahoma, surrounded by devastation, one can feel the innocence. A word for the ground? Blessed.

Overly poetic, yeah, but this tiny arrival had that effect. Our trailer park became a campground of news vans and satellite dishes. The story of the airborne baby with raven-black hair hypnotized our state and eclipsed other storm-related news, such as the destruction of the aforementioned prison and the disappearance of several fearsome inmates. But looking back, Gullary got it right. Violent escapees weren't nearly as unnerving as this one, beautiful girl.

At least to me.

Great lengths were taken to discover the child's rightful home. Claims on a clock, a cow, and a baby girl were few, and the fistful that did come in ended up bogus. Days turned to months, and finally the courthouse spoke. Ms. P was granted rightful guardianship, and added another to her family.

"Look at that peacock." Ma hissed the words beneath her breath whenever she saw our neighbor outside with her three-year-old son, Connor, and the dubiously obtained child.

"I was given the feet of that babe. I should've had say in the choice of a decent name."

Ma's opinion never did change. In fact, she blamed the name for much of what followed. But I'd say Ms. Pickering pegged Miracle Baby with the only name that made sense, given her unique arrival.

Stormi.

CHAPTER 1

One week after the storm, Ma planted a cottonwood out front of our trailer. She later explained it as an act of defiance. Ma was sinking roots, declaring that no tornado could dislodge our family from Green Country, the eastern wedge of Oklahoma infiltrated by the Ozark's mountainous tentacles.

Defiance or not, the cottonwood was woefully out of place. Gullary nestled in the Henshaw Valley astride Gullary Creek, which flowed easily from Lake Gullary set higher up and on the far side of the Arkansas border. Oak and Black Hickory found the creek and our town to their liking. Aside from Ms. Harrison's renegade apple tree, Gullary tolerated no other varieties.

"So why'd you have to plant a cottonwood?" I asked Mom this every spring, when the cottony fluff set my eyes to watering.

"You understand the principle of sowing and reaping. All these wispy seeds will take flight, take root, and one day change the look of this valley."

"You don't like how it looks?"

Mom never answered that. She'd eye that cottonwood, and the seeds swirling in the wind. "Sowing and reaping, Jonah, it's inevitable. A law of God."

My first photos of that tree evidenced a slender shoot, aiming straight for the sky. But somewhere along the way, its trunk had second thoughts and took a detour. The tree twisted, gnarled.

Bent.

But the cottonwood still grew leaves, broad leaves that fell green and full and hid the abnormal growth, and Ma called it lovely.

I have no leaves.

And it may not be a law of God, but the law of teen-hood is near as unshakable: senior year doesn't hide anything.

"This way, folks." I stepped in front of the mural, beneath the "Gullary's Glorious History" sign. While the most recent addition to the tornado museum, this display was also the ugliest—Kelli McCann's best fifth-grade, sidewalk-chalk effort at a prison, a twister, and a little cradle.

I reached into my back pocket and removed my cheat sheet. It had been so long since we snagged a visitor, I forgot most all of my fancy lines. I cleared my throat, peeked at my notes, and plastered a stupid smile on my face.

"Our town was once known for more than storms and babies dropping from the sky. Long before that night, Gullary meant lead—lead and zinc, but also chat, the pulverized, toxic leftovers we dug up and then dumped. Like nearby towns, mining placed Gullary on the map, and then blasted a hole beneath it.

"Sinkholes ate buildings. Slides trapped miners. And a bustling town nestled into the Ozarks gave up its soul. Fifteen thousand mining jobs packed up and left, along with the scratchers willing to drop into that hell."

I paused for dramatic effect and gestured around the museum.

"It happened all over. Treece. Cardin. Picher . . . where sky-blue Tar Creek turned red with iron. Contaminated. Poisoned. Dead. And when people leave, Feds always come. They declared our town a toxic waste site.

"But here in Gullary, a few hundred people remained. A few hundred very determined people, including my grand-parents. A handful of folks and a whole lot of chat.

"Those two hills, the chat piles you likely saw on your way in, still stand as reminder of what happens when you dig too deep. 'In Gullary, the past best stay buried.' Those were my granddad's words."

I moved on and tapped the black-and-white picture of four grim miners, emerging from their hole with their faces covered in grime.

"Now, I mention Gullary's mining ghosts because it explains this town's reaction when the Feds first threw us a lifeline in the form of a new Supermax prison facility, SMX for short. Hundreds of the most violent criminals on earth moved into our neighborhood. You'd think it would cause fear.

"Not here in Gullary. We saw the promise of jobs, and lots of them. Soon we all relied on SMX—my ma was the cook—and Gullary was reborn on the shoulders of rapists and murderers." I scratched my head and shrugged. "Strange way to bring life back to a town."

My tourist couple exchanged glances, and the wife cleared her throat. "And then the tornadoes came?"

"Not right away, but yeah, we can't catch a break." I gestured toward the next photo, a snapshot of the largest funnel, taken by Greasy Jake while crouched behind his garage's dumpster. The twister bore down in the background while a hubcap took flight in the fore. Priceless.

"An F5," I said. "Nothing survives a direct hit from an F5."

"But those chat piles out there did. You did." Wife let her gaze travel my frame. "Is that how you, I mean, did that tornado bend your . . . oh, I'm not sure how to say it."

Husband grabbed her arm and glared. "Then don't. You don't ask about personal matters." He turned to me. "Sorry, your situation's none of ours."

I gritted my teeth, and crumpled up my lines. "No. Storms don't give kids scoliosis."

It was time to conclude this tour.

"The first of many tiny twisters struck at bedtime eighteen years ago, pushing most of the town underground. Our people survived that night, but the prison didn't. Usually, F5s take everything. But this one was different. It had . . . mercy. When that monster landed, it seemed bound and determined to claim only one thing, the complex. Once it wiped the foundation clean, it stopped on a dime and turned back the way it came. In the aftermath, the chat piles were undisturbed, but not one stone of this former building was left on another. The crews couldn't even find the remains of most of the inmates.

We needed jobs, so we rebuilt it, but the government cut funding, and SMX never reopened. Now here it sits. A fully operational Supermax prison that houses only this small tornado museum, and employs exactly one person: me." I opened the front door and peeked toward the courtyard. "Well, that's it."

I placed my mouth on autopilot. "If you've enjoyed your tour today, please consider a gift to Gullary's Tornado Gallery." I gestured toward the plastic, coin-collecting funnel. "Any contribution is mighty appreciated."

The gentleman smiled and dug in his pocket, pulling out two twenties. His wife gasped and slapped his shoulder, but he stepped toward me and shook the bills. "Life can't be easy all bent like that, and I want to tip you, but first, I've been curious about something the whole time. This entire joint is white and gray . . ." He pointed over his shoulder. "Except for that. What's behind the bright red door?"

I exhaled long and slow. For forty bucks, I'd tell him I wet the bed until twelve years old, and that I spent hours gawking at photos of Stormi. I'd name every drunk in town, and whisper the places they go when the moon is full. For a tip, any tip, I'd spill all of Gullary's secrets.

But I couldn't tell him what was behind the red door.

"Sorry." I shook my head and forced a smile. "You now know more about Gullary than some of its residents. Best keep one detail private."

He tongued his cheek, and gave the bills a final shake before stuffing them into his pocket. "Fair enough."

I stood in the doorway and watched my money walk out the main entrance—past the guardhouse, through the electric fencing—and vanish beneath the wide Oklahoma sky.

First visitor in a month, and so close to getting a tip for my time.

I sighed and shook my head. Describing pictures in a one-room tornado museum barely hinted at employment, but in Gullary, few eighteen-year-olds could boast of any income, so I never complained. Final exams and our upcoming graduation did little to brighten the future. Gullary was a house of mirrors. Everyone thought they knew a way out, but decades later, all the same faces remained.

I spun back into the museum and slammed the door behind me, breathing in the bought air. I peeked at the clock. 12:30.

"Lunchtime."

I lifted a tray from beneath the counter and removed the plastic wrap. Ma went all out today: fried chicken, mashed potatoes, gravy, and cranberries.

Too bad it wasn't for me.

I gentled aside my 35mm camera and grabbed my crushed brown bag, offering an exaggerated eye roll. Likely the usual: knockoff peanut butter and Aunt Josephine's tangerine jam.

I carried both lunches toward the red door and paused. This part of my job description never felt right. Stormi always said danger lurked where I was about to go, and I, more than most, knew the folly of ignoring her prophesies.

But in this matter, I had no choice.

Though heavy metal, the door swung open easily, and I slipped inside. Leaning into it with my knee, I slid a brick along the floor and propped it open. But that much steel had a will of its own. I stepped away and listened as the weight pushed that brick right out. It closed with a clank, and my shoulders slumped. I wouldn't be leaving the way I came in. There was no keyhole or handle—not on this side—and I stared down the well-lit hall.

"Locked in SMX. I don't get paid enough."

"That you, Jonah? You're late." Ahead, a pair of hands waved me nearer.

"Yeah. I got held up. A couple lost tourists wandered into the gallery." I marched forward, stopping in front of cell 117. Tres's cell.

"Boy, you know a geezer like me got needs. If you have visitors, they need to clear out of my house before twelve thirty. I thought we had that straight."

"Sometimes prisoners don't get their way."

Tres whistled. "Ain't that the truth?"

How do you tell museum visitors that the Gullary town council secretly keeps a guy locked up behind the red door? I'd never found the words to work it into my presentation, especially as I wasn't sure why myself. I asked Dad my first day; right after Ma handed me two dinners.

"Jonah, I'm not at liberty to discuss the matter. That's Circle business. But as the Max's only employee, your responsibilities include mowing the grass and feeding Tres, its only prisoner."

"At least tell me what he did. Am I feeding a serial killer? Some Hannibal Lector/*Silence of the Lambs* type? You do know I'm there alone with the guy."

"Do the job. I don't expect you to understand." Dad winced and slapped my back, as if I had a lot of growing up to do. "You're just a boy."

After that first shift at SMX, I locked up the joint and beelined it to Greasy Jake's Garage. Stormi was there, working late. Without pay.

"Just a boy, huh?" Stormi handed me her wrench and straightened. "Your dad's a piece of work." She folded her arms. "Ever seen such a beauty?"

"No."

I was supposed to be admiring the engine, but as usual my gaze was fixed on Stormi. She was my own age—at least that was our best guess, given her appearance upon arrival—however, similarities stopped there. There was a confidence that animated her words. She was free, free and wild. Gullary had no hold on her. It felt like she was here by choice, which made no sense. Whatever seed grows certainty had taken deep root.

"Jonah?"

I blinked free and shifted my gaze toward the hood. "It's a cheap V6 engine," I said.

"Look beyond that. She came to me as a monster. She's a kitten now."

Stormi was Jake's right hand. In truth, she was both of his hands. No car could hide its mystery ailments from her, and after two years of her dedicated employment, Jake owned the only garage in town and was a very wealthy man. Wealthy enough that he could spend his days with his new shoes kicked up on his new desk playing his newest video game while Stormi ran the place.

"Did you know there was a guy locked up in the Max?"

She reached for a rag and wiped her hands.

"Am I the only one who didn't? Why is he in there? I mean, what if he's some psycho person-eater who could hypnotize me and trick me into opening his cell—"

"He's not a zombie." Stormi took firm hold of my cheeks, then released. She bit her lip, dipped the rag in mineral spirits, and dabbed at the smudges on my face. "He's an old guy who's been there forever."

"What did he do?"

"I don't know. Something awful, I'm sure." She threw down the rag. "You need to feed him, right? You can do that. Just walk in, drop off the food, and walk out. Like you're feeding a puppy. Without the petting." She grinned and I didn't and she exhaled. "Listen, I don't know why he's there. I know it's for a reason, so don't, you know, do what you do."

"Which is what, exactly?"

"You listen to people and believe them and then you get hurt."

"So, I'm naïve." I stepped back and folded my arms. "You're calling me naïve. Just a boy. Same as Dad."

Stormi was silent and shifted on her feet.

"That's not me," I continued. "And it's not fair. You know I don't trust *him*."

"Well, your dad's a piece of work. I don't see how your ma puts up with it. But he's only one in a very big world."

I paused. "Connor!" Silly how triumphant I felt at the remembering. "I don't trust your brother either. So that's two."

Stormi leaned over the hood, her voice suddenly tired. "Add the prisoner to that list and you'll be fine."

I opened my eyes and shook free from the memory. I'd kept my guard up for about a week, but time slowly whittles away concern. Tres was perpetually good-spirited. I enjoyed his company. But Stormi's words plagued me when our visits became lengthy. Stormi was never wrong, while I rarely had ideas of my own. Ignoring her never sat well with me.

Tres smacked his parched lips. "What did Lizza cook on up? Oh, Lord!" His eyes grew. "It must be Thanksgiving. Is it Thanksgiving, son?"

I slid Tres's food into his cell and took my seat in the chair across the hall. We were in the only well-lit section of SMX. Here, locked behind traditional bars, a prisoner felt much less confined, unlike the rest of the units, where solid steel doors and a four-inch window were the norm. Tres flourished in minimum security, or so Dad said.

"No. But the thought of you must've brought Ma extreme joy. You are experiencing last night's leftovers, and the meal was incredible. I tried for a second helping, but she whacked my hand with a ladle. 'Jonah,' she said, 'you best learn now to leave some for the unfortunates in this world.' That always means you. Now, when it comes to me, Ma's extreme joy must disappear." I shook my brown bag in the air. "Peanut butter again."

Tres paused, his fork halfway to half a set of teeth. "Growin' boy like you? You know I'm willing to make a barter—"

"No, you go on. Remember, that's both lunch and supper. I can't complain. Besides, you don't own anything I need."

I glanced around Tres's cell. Bed, toilet, desk, books, and chessboard.

My chessboard.

A gift from Stormi, but I'd never learned to play. At least now it was getting use.

19

My gaze landed on Tres and I chewed and stared and chewed some more. I put him at seventy, but it never felt right to question. He was tall, and built with enough muscle to cause apprehension. Tres said he was nothing but a drifter; he said we were doing him a great kindness by providing him food and shelter. I couldn't figure out how a drifter could be happy locked up, living a solitary life, but here again I never probed. I rarely had the chance. Our lunch talks focused on only two people: Stormi and me.

"That girl of yours is comin' up near eighteen, if I'm right." Tres gnawed on a drumstick.

That girl of yours? I wish.

I took a mouthful of sandwich. "It's kind of hard to say, given that she didn't blow in with papers or a birth certificate. We'll go out for ice cream again on July fifth, seeing as Ms. P never sees fit to celebrate."

"Still." Tres swiped grease from his mouth. "I'm certain her actual eighteenth is coming up. Does she look it?"

"I don't really follow what you're asking—"

"Oh, sure you do, fool. Is she pretty?" Tres showed his teeth. "Like me."

I started to rock in my chair. "Well, pretty doesn't really touch it. I won't go into what *you* are, but Stormi—"

"Finish that, now." Tres scooted forward on his bunk. "You usually don't make it this far. But Stormi what?"

It's not like the truth would go anywhere; it'd bounce around a cell with an old man.

"If you could see her. She walks into a room, a packed room, and suddenly she's in hyper focus, and everyone and everything else blurs in the background. And then she looks at you, and her image gets sharper still. But you can't hold her gaze long, and just like that you realize you're gawking at her lips or neck or . . ." I cleared my throat. "Maybe I'll bring a picture sometime."

"I'd like that. Very much."

I stared off down the hallway. "She knows me, knows pretty much everything. Maybe everything."

"Everything? That's a poor stratagem. Strapping lad like you must have the ladies falling at your feet." Tres gently placed his tray on his bed, and his voice softened. "Trusting everything to only one puts a man at a disadvantage."

"Disadvantage? I know her better than anyone. And she shares everything with me too, so it's not one-sided, or not totally one-sided. I don't think." I glanced down. "But we're close. In every way except for . . ." A heavy sigh escaped. "Except for the way she's close to other guys."

It gets really quiet.

"But what should I expect, right?" I tried to straighten, and winced as my back screamed. "Why would she want to be with deformed me?"

Tres scratched his head. "What do you mean 'other guys'?"

I slapped the floor. "You need it spelled out? She goes out. A lot. And when those guys fill the locker room with their talk, I can't bear to stick around and listen. But based on the number of times her name flies around, I can only imagine she's probably not saying no too often. To anyone. Not that I know for sure, I mean, how could I know? No. Oh no." My fingers tingled. "Oh, God."

My eyes blurred, and I slowly lowered myself to the floor. The ringing in my ears overpowered.

A seizure was knocking on my door.

"Jonah, calm down, kid. I was just clarify . . . What's go . . . on . . . ?"

My hearing muddled and Tres's syllables fought through in staccato bursts. The chair slid away, and my body curled, fixed and fetal, on the ground.

I fought my fit for a while, like I always did. I searched for something that made sense, something clear, but when my vision failed and my right eye fell blind, I let the monster inside have its way with me.

Idiot seizure. Leave me alone.

It wouldn't, not for another twenty minutes of mouth-foaming, eye-fluttering misery. I was kidnapped, whipped by the brain meant to serve me. My hands clawed and my head jerked rhythmically against the tile floor.

I felt nothing.

But I heard.

Screams. Girl screams. Boy screams. Ghostly shrieks. A seizure had never brought such terror with it before.

And then feeling returned. A warm breeze swept over me, and the rhythm of my head slowed. Another minute, and I lay face down, gasping, my back aching, but my body and mind at rest.

The room stilled. My seizure had gone. But not my tears—they puddled on the tile.

"You okay, kid?" Tres's voice was gentle. "You done beat yourself up pretty good."

It would be minutes until my legs supported me, and I uncurled and stared at the ceiling. I touched my face, splotched with a combination of nose blood and peanut butter.

"I'll be all right. Happens once a week or so. Old Rickety decided to interrupt our lunch, is all. I'm surprised he hasn't taken me in here before now." I wiped my eyes and forced my head to the side, and frowned. In my distress, I had traveled clear across the hall. My shoulder pressed against cell 119, the one that neighbored Tres's. A chill worked its way around my neck and weaved down my twisted spine. I glanced back at Tres, his face visible in the mirror he held out through the bars.

"How'd I get over here?"

"You scooted, all jerky-like. Old Rickety? That was a seizure, right?" Tres set his mirror down on the table. "Why did you name it?"

I fired a glance into the empty cell, the one that spooks me whenever I pass. "You can't hate something that doesn't have a name."

"Oh, I don't know about that. I do know your brain and your bend must weigh as heavy burdens. I also know life ain't fair. These next days'll be hard on this town. Cryin' shame that a good kid like you should have to pay for what's been done." Tres clasped his hands on the outside of the bars.

"'What's been done'?" Even in a post-seizure fog, the words struck as ominous.

"Jonah, you've been right kind to me. Since your first day, you've treated me well. I took notice, son. It's been noticed. Remember that." Tres spoke quietly, so quietly I wasn't sure if his voice came from the inside or the outside of my head. "Don't be afraid."

Understand that in Gullary, biblical admonitions floated around like cottonwood fluff. Tossed liberally into earthly conversations, like table salt, so overused they lost their impact. Unfortunate, really.

"Maybe next time, let's keep our conversations about Stormi." I pushed up to a sit. "It's preferable to this little morbid path you're walking."

"You're right. I'm sorry, son." Tres's strong baritone returned. "But, now, get on up if you can. You done your piece with me, and the gallery needs ya. I'm figurin' you'll have a visitor waiting."

"Two tours in a day? Not likely." I raised myself to my feet, picked up the chair, and glanced at the mess on the floor. "I'll be back to clean this tomorrow. You okay with that?"

Tres smiled. "Oh, and next time you see her, tell Stormi hello, and, if you would, give her this." He opened his desk drawer and pulled out a necklace, gold and beautiful. He stroked it and then reached it out to me. "Seeing as I'm in here and she's not, I'm thinkin' she'd probably not accept it if'n she knew where it came from, but maybe if you was puttin' thought on a birthday gift, it could come from you. But it's your call." He sighed. "Nothin' asked, nothin' required."

I stared at the necklace. "It's really . . . wow, it's um . . . but how did you get it, and why would you, and all that?"

"Shut up and take the necklace."

"She'll know this wasn't from me. She always seems to know."

"Take it!" He closed his eyes, and his voice softened. "Try. For me. For you. While you can still head it off."

Looking back, Tres left a breadcrumb trail clear enough to follow through the thickest of the Ozarks. No, I don't reckon I could have pieced it all together, but I should have recognized the puzzle. Unfortunately, hurry, perception's greatest enemy, had me by the neck.

He dropped the necklace and a napkin into my hand. "You might want to use them both."

I sighed at the mess I'd made, and the mess I'd become.

"Say, kid, do me one more favor." He gestured at my chessboard. "Get your brainiac friend's next move—the quicker the better." Tres took a deep breath. "This match is takin' too long. It's been days since you've brought me Arthur's play. Not much else to look forward to, if you get my meaning." He walked over, lifted a pawn, and slowly waved it in the air. "We're entering the endgame, you know." He gazed into me and then closed his eyes.

"Who is?" I asked. "You and Arthur?"

"We all are, Jonah. We all are."

My exit involved a slow weave through the most controlled section of the prison to the opposite end, where the magnetic card in my pocket would free me through the service door. Though my vertebrae balked at the distance, I knew I could gut it through; I'd locked myself in before.

Which is why I knew the terror of cell 119. How could an empty cell create such dread? I hadn't a clue, but that chamber was evil, as sure as the day was long.

A bit of history: Reconstruction of the SMX had spared no detail. Following the twister, it was reborn, a twin to the original. The first prison had four wings, as did the second. The first, four courtyards, as did the second. The first, two hundred cells—two hundred sequentially numbered cells.

But here another breadcrumb fell unconsidered. The rebuild tweaked the cell numbers. There was no cell 118. It had been skipped, like floor thirteen of a hotel, and the over-sized unit was given the number 119 instead.

A little thing. Probably an oversight. No big deal.

Except that the misnumbered cell always felt dark. Foul.

Chilling enough to send a post-seizure tremor through my body.

I lumbered away from Tres and the cell that haunted me, and emerged at the far end of the prison. It was a warm fifteen-minute walk around the perimeter back to the front entrance. I didn't travel it alone; those screaming voices still echoed in my head.

I shook them free and hurried to the museum door, which stood ajar.

I peeked inside. Stormi slid off the counter and swept back her hair, brushing back the few dark strands that clung to her lips. Her hair was wild—not unkempt, just wild—and her complexion tanned. Surrounded by all that smooth darkness, her white teeth glimmered. "I got here as fast as I could." She cocked her head and let her gaze roam my face. "Peanut butter again. Looks like I'm a little late."

"You're never late. Admit it: You were out here when I was seizing in there. You could've come in." I stared at her hard and unforgiving, noticed her penitent sadness, and kept on. I had a goodly reservoir of righteous anger. "If you had, there would be no blood and no peanut butter, and maybe I would have heard your voice instead of screams."

She exhaled, and my hot air balloon floated gently back down to earth.

"I can't figure out why Tres frightens you," I said. "He's locked behind bars. He's forever old. A puppy. You told me yourself."

She stepped up and wiped my chin with her thumb, her touch setting my body on fire. "You don't have to believe everything I say. Listen, can we get out of here?" Her face brightened. "I have a surprise for you, so grab your camera. I'm inviting you to a private birthday party."

That girl of yours is coming up on eighteen.

I bit my lip and peeked at the red door. "Your real birthday. You think it's coming up soon?"

"Today." She kissed my cheek. "Eighteen today."

CHAPTER 2

I followed Stormi out of SMX and round Windy Road. A word on Gullary: US-59 brings you in, US-59 leads you out. But if you're willing to risk your life, there were plenty of smaller routes out of town.

One being Windy Road.

As the name suggested, it twisted its spongy finger deep into the Springfield Plateau. Thin, overgrown with forest, and blocked when the rains came, it was a path rarely followed. I'd walked it as far as the Gullary-Green River split, though not without considerable lumbar discomfort. Beyond that, though only two miles from my home, the Windy went rogue and became an uneven trail.

With a brain eager to rise up and throw me to my knees, the river always seemed a safe place to stop.

"Keep up, Jonah! I'll be nineteen by the time we get there."

"How come suddenly you know your birthdate for certain? Another prophetess moment? You never knew your birthday before."

Stormi glanced back over her shoulder, smooth and tanned in that green strapless top that hugged so well.

"No. This is different. This year I *feel* my birthday. I felt it when I woke up, and by noon there was no doubt." Stormi shrugged. "It's today."

How does anyone feel a birthday?

She reached the moss bridge over the Green, slowing to gloat with a voice full and free. "You're always falling behind."

I slowed further still. "If you'd told me we were going to walk into Arkansas, I'd have stolen the truck. I've no desire to hike that far."

Stormi gripped the bridge railing, her body swaying back and forth. Hair splashed down on those shoulders and once again I knew: I would follow my best friend anywhere.

"Then how far do you want to go on my birthday?" She cocked her head and licked those flawless lips.

Don't answer that. You always lose this game.

"Jonah?"

You listen, you believe, and then you get hurt.

"Are you talking distance, or are you talking how far, you know, well, when a normal girl asks a normal guy that . . ." My voice lowered to a mumble. "I don't mean that you're abnormal, but a person might think you were asking about something more personal or physical or . . ."

Her eyes were wide, but her face gave away nothing.

"You know, maybe let's forget this last minute. I thought maybe that was a real you-and-me question, but I can see on your face . . . I can't see anything on your face. Let's go to Arkansas."

It's hard to love your best friend. Over the years, the Line of Friendship is drawn, thickened, deepened, until it becomes a freakin' canyon. Maybe if I would have grabbed her hand early on, in kindergarten, before my back twisted and my brain rebelled. Maybe that would have built a bridge to get across.

But time solidifies the status quo. It was too late, and I was stuck on my side, lobbing idiotic emotions across the chasm, hoping she'd bite. I couldn't tell if she saw me as friend or beast or charity case, but it didn't matter.

I only needed her to stick around.

I raised the camera from my chest and focused the lens on Stormi. She smiled broadly, and I zoomed in and took a perfect shot. Definitely a bedroom-wall keeper.

"We're almost there, Jonah." Stormi's eyes were pure light. "The spot is right ahead."

She bounded across the river, turning to wait on the far side. I took a deep breath and approached the moss bridge, some twenty feet above the water. My head lightened. It would be a bad site for a seizure.

The river hadn't always caused dread.

Not when we were young. Second-grade young.

Strange that our parents let us wander as they did; seven years old and we had the run of town and beyond, though how far we strayed remained our secret. We loved the moss bridge for the elven realm we were certain lay across it, hidden deep in the forest. Like all kids in Gullary, we were fantasy junkies, dreaming of worlds far away. We watched *The Fellowship of the Ring* until we could recite the lines, until they were no longer fantasy, until they became our own. Stormi was Arwen from the House of Elrond, and I was her Aragorn.

I saved her from a thousand restless orcs, rescued her from Sauron's clutches time and again. And once, while splashing about in the river, my heel brushed against a small, smooth object in the sand. I dived down and emerged with a ring.

It was rusty, but we scrubbed it until it glinted silver in the sunlight.

"You found the Ring." Stormi's eyes grew. "The ring of power."

My thoughts always tilted a bit more toward reality. "I think it's just an old ring."

"No." She shook her head solemnly, and reached the prize back toward me. "It's yours to keep. When you're in trouble, you'll need it."

"Nah. Take it."

She thought a moment, and slipped it over her thumb.

The next day, Stormi arrived at the bridge and held out a necklace. "I'm giving this to you." It was her shark's tooth on a leather string.

"Why are you giving me your—"

"It's in the movie, stupid. Arwen gives Aragorn her necklace. It's like a heart."

"It's like a tooth."

She kicked my shin and tied the leather string around my neck. It never did come off.

After the discovery of the ring, our Hobbit dramas became more extravagant. Stormi would toss the ring from the bridge, and I would dive in after it, reviving hope and saving Middle Earth.

And then, July five happened. Stormi was eight, and I was late to our adventure. Ma had me cleaning my room, and I reached the bridge in time to hear the splash. Stormi had jumped.

I dove in after, because for all Stormi could do, the girl could not swim. I found her a foot beneath the surface and dragged her to shore.

She coughed and sputtered. "Get my ring!"

And I did. I saved both her and the world, which were basically synonymous.

In time, our Hobbit games faded, until last month.

"Remember when I used to throw my ring." Stormi had leaned over the bridge's edge. "You always found it."

"Yeah," I called up from the bank.

Stormi bit her lip, removed the old band from the finger it still rounded, and tossed it in. "Save me, Jonah. For old times."

"Seriously?"

She gave no answer.

I exhaled, stood, and waded gingerly into the river. Three steps, and the seizure took me, threw me back onto the bank. When I came to, Stormi had not moved. She stared down at me, her face disappointed.

"I'll get it." She dove and soon swam toward me, ring in hand. She never wore it again.

How far I'd fallen.

But now, eager to forget recent failures, I followed her. Old Rickety had mercy, and once again Stormi laughed and took off running. I set out in hot pursuit, a term you'd deem mighty generous had you seen my lurch. I stumbled around the bend and barreled into her.

I tried gamely to both keep her upright and hold myself vertical, but it was an either/or. My spine landed hard on a gnarled tree root.

Stormi knelt, wincing at my misfortune. "That was very sweet."

"Oh," I groaned. "The part where I crushed you or the part where I crushed me?"

"Both. But more than the crushing, you kept me standing."

There are few conditions that render a body more infantile than a bad back. Should you hear of someone complaining of the ailment, it ought to immediately draw forth all manner of sympathetic prayer. The pain is akin to a knife, plunged deep into bone and marrow, and then twisted, once and again. I tried to shift, to rise to an elbow, but the blade twisted, and I rejoined the earth. Stormi laid a hand on my chest. "Don't. Stay there." She lifted my head onto her lap, and gently stroked the dirt from my arms, my shirt. Her hair swished across my face while her hands paused above my heart.

Had this been the first time I'd felt her healing touch, I'd have endured agony and flipped over quick so as to hide the sudden and dramatic effect she had on certain personal parts of me, but I had spent considerable time with my head on her lap in the past, recovering from a seizure's sudden arrival.

This is because of her "knowing," and perhaps here is a good time to clarify. There is a knowing borne of experience. Old Gantry used fifty years of this variety of understanding to turn fishing on Lake Gullary into a pitiful affair. Those fish had no chance. Stormi possessed no such insight; she owned *foresight*, a frightening ability to see beyond experienced time. Her mind's reach into the future extended into most matters, but when it came to me, it stretched farther. She knew when Old Rick was coming, knew where I was, knew how to find me. Stormi saved my life multiple times after my brain threw me down in places wild and remote. Stormi was my soldier, the one battling the creature caged in my skull. Though I wanted her more than life itself, maybe it was best not to disturb our delicate friendship balance.

Even if her smile filled every pleasant dream.

Minutes later, the grip on my lumbar eased, and I hauled myself up. "Well, lead on. I don't know where we're going."

"We're here. This is it. This is where I wanted to celebrate. With you."

"On this path?" I lowered myself back down to my knees.

She glanced around, shrugged, and nodded.

"But we fell by chance. This can't be what you had in mind."

"I don't believe in chance." Stormi dug into the front pocket of her cutoffs. "You know what I want? What I've never had?"

No, but I'm willing to oblige.

She yanked out her hand. In it, a pink candle and a book of matches. "I want a wish. I'm eighteen, and you know my mom's paranoia about celebrations, and I can live with that, but a girl can't live without making a wish."

I grinned. "No, I'd say that's mandatory." I grabbed a stick and twisted it into the dirt, pressed the candle into the hole, and mounded dirt around its base. "Allow me."

Soon Stormi's eyes glinted in the light of a tiny flame.

"Now close your eyes," I said. "That's right. And make your wish. But you can't tell me what it is."

"Thank you for the tutorial." Stormi cracked an eyelid. "Did you really think I was going to?" She squeezed her eyes shut and blew.

Flame out.

"Can I tell you my wish after it comes true?" she asked.

While that seemed unnecessary, I acquiesced. I sat and watched the wisp of smoke rise from the candle and circle around Stormi. A minute later I risked her gaze. She stared at me and my eyes darted.

"Hold me."

I raised my brows and pointed at myself.

She nodded slowly.

I started to scoot near and then paused. "Have you ever knocked down dominoes?"

"What?"

"You know, set them up in a row and pushed the first over and then watched all of them tumble?"

"No, I haven't."

"That may be the problem. See, in dominoes, there is a trajectory. Things go down in a specific direction. You set 'm up, push the first, and the others fall in order. I think what you and I are missing is trajectory."

"Trajectory," she repeated.

I repositioned my spine, summoning all the courage I owned. "We're together a lot, you and me. A *lot*. But it feels like maybe some dominoes haven't been knocked down, some key relational dominoes."

"Relational dominoes."

"Yeah, relational dominoes. It's as if we've been playing a chance game like Yahtzee, when we should have been playing dominoes. It seems, at least from what I can tell, when a guy and girl spend this much time together there usually comes a first push, a noticing—you know, interest. That starts the trajectory."

"Fascinating analogy." She reached out and stroked my hair. "So first the push of interest. And then?"

"Well, then might come a more tangible event between them, maybe an event that makes the interest very, very clear."

"Hmm." She leaned forward, crawling slowly toward me. Her arms rounded my shoulders and she eased in, whispering, her lips brushing my ear. "Next domino, please."

I wriggled. "This is the problem. The next domino might be a bigger deal, you know, that they would remember for a long time. Sort of a key—intimate, if you want to use the

37

word—only-between-them kind of domino. But between us, this domino won't fall over. And I get it, I mean . . ." Her warm breath caressed my neck and I gathered my thoughts, lost them, and picked up what I could.

"Why should you want to knock over a domino with a bloody, peanut-butter-covered me? It's just that when you say stuff like 'hold me,' this stupid domino can't figure out what you want from it, er, him, I mean me."

"I see. How about this? When she says 'hold me,' she wants you to hold her."

"And uh, that's it, right?" I bowed slightly, resting my forehead against hers. "Hold you. Our game ends in a holding pattern. Nothing falls after that?"

Stormi thought for a moment. "How long does it usually take for all the dominoes to fall?"

"Normally, it happens pretty quick."

"That's the problem," she said softly, and caressed my chest with her cheek. "Wait for me."

This was not fair. This was agonizing. If you've ever been banished to the friend zone—which holds confusions similar to the twilight zone—and the perfect object of your desire presses into you, you know this wasn't fair, not even on a birthday. But I didn't dispute. Right there on that path, for the first time, a piece of my own wish was granted, and I reached my arms around Stormi and drew her tight. As the sun stretched long shadows over the Ozarks, and the evening breezes brought with them the scent and rustle of hickory, I still held her. We lay on that dirt path, every now and then her body shifting against mine.

For a deformed epileptic, I guess this is as good as it gets.

Stormi nuzzled my neck and whispered words imperceptible. With anyone else, this would be a beginning, but with me it marked an end, and no matter how much my heart ached, I would not ask for more. She was at peace; I felt it, though I did not know why, and I daydreamed into a memory.

CHAPTER 3

I recalled last December's annual spinal measurement. One of the few times I'd ignored Stormi. The doctor had placed his hands on my twisted, leafless trunk.

"Twenty-one degrees forward, ten degrees to the left. The bend is accelerating. It's like I've been telling you." He scratched his chin and then his balding scalp, likely pondering all manner of delicate words. But he was speaking to Dad. No gentle message would do. "Jonah's back is a sight to behold. Never seen such a dramatic case of scoliosis."

That word always sounded sinister. Maybe the Latin name for a dying tree, like *E. deforma monstrus freakosis*, or some ancient curse like *Forevis Screwediosis Bendicus*.

"Please. Take the young man's warped back to Mayo." Dr. Only-Doctor-in-Gullary-Who'd-Never-Before-Seen-a-Back-Like-Mine exhaled hard in Dad's direction. "And best sooner than later. My guess? They'll crack it, rod it . . . who knows, maybe fuse it. I've heard young bone grows fine around rods and bolts."

Mom teared up and Dad frowned down and I tried my darnedest to sit straight. *Screwediosis Bendicus*? A rotten lot, but survivable. The thought of young bone—*my* young bone—fusing around parts from Lurvy's Hardware?

Pretty much the end of the world.

Turned out, Armageddon was quick in coming. The operation schedule was determined. And so was Stormi, right up until the night before the trip.

"Don't let him take you." Stormi pressed into my shoulder, shivering in the night. From where we sat on my family's front step, the moon hung orange and low, a glop of color clinging to a black canvas. It looked about to fall.

"Why are you telling me this the night before?" I peeked down at her face. My, Stormi had turned out beautiful.

"Because if you go tomorrow, if you go through with this, everything will get worse."

"Pretty cataclysmic sentiment, Stormi. You see the curve. I'm not thinking worse is possible."

She drew a breath and rose, lingered on the top step, staring across the lawn at her trailer. "Why do you think I landed here?"

"I was pretty young. I didn't get a chance to ask the tornado. But I'm not sure why we're talking about you right now. Can't we focus on my trip and how everything's going to be fine, and my spine is finally going to be straight—"

"It's not your stupid back I'm worried about." Stormi's voice was flat, emotionless.

"What then?" I jumped up and grabbed her shoulder. "Are they going to screw up some procedure and leave me vegetated?"

She turned, faced me, reached out, and held my cheeks in her hands. "Procedure? Oh, Jonah, you won't make it that far."

"Okay, this time I need you to explain your little premonition, 'cause you're talking death language, and if there's one thing I do not need to hear, it's death language, not the night before."

She squeezed me tight. "It's my turn to wait for you." Stormi backed down the steps, turned, and stepped slowly toward her trailer home. "Someday you'll return the favor."

I cupped my hands and called, "You'll wait for a happy, living me or a not-so-cheery, dead-type me?"

Stormi paused at her door. "Both." Her door clicked shut behind her.

From anyone else, I'd have chalked up her concern to over-protection. But when Stormi gave a prediction, you didn't bet against her, and you certainly didn't risk it.

Not after she brought flowers to Jason Murphy's house ten minutes *before* two military officers arrived to give the tragic news of Jason's sacrifice.

Not after she invited Ashley for a sleepover the same night a gas line explosion leveled her friend's double-wide.

You didn't question Stormi. I, especially, should've known.

Yet, pain tilts otherwise reasonable thought. Under duress, I understand why prisoners spill their secrets to the enemy. Unrelenting agony overshadowed Stormi's words, and I climbed into bed after she left, falling asleep to thoughts of flagpoles and skyscrapers—proud, straight things. I would soon be counted among them.

On Christmas Day, Ma kissed both my cheeks European style, and Dad and I climbed into the 1984 Ford F-150. We chugged six hundred mostly silent miles north to the Mayo Clinic in Rochester, Minnesota.

That trip to Minnesota was cold. Stupid cold. Inside and outside the truck.

My "correction" began with what hospital folks called a work-up—or, better put, *Testicus-up-the-Butticus*. There were CAT scans and PET scans and MRI scans. After all that scanning, we consulted with ten different doctors, none with a sense of humor, and each with the word *neuro* in his or her title. Meeting with *neuro*surgeons—people who sawed skulls and poked brains—made me want to vomit.

Those doctors put their humorless heads together and developed my "treatment plan." That term sounded so gentle, so nurturing.

Don't believe it. It's code for freaking *surgery*, likely the first of many. Turns out Dr. Only-Doctor-in-Gullary was dead-on. My treatment plan included a violent spine crack, five vertebra shaves, cartilage rips, a hip bone harvest, and finally a white-knuckled fusion. Add a few rods and pins and, in three months, I would be titanium straight.

Hallelujah.

The afternoon before found me lying in bed, fiddling with my 35mm, taking random shots of the bedpan and flower arrangement on my bedside table.

"Jonah Everett the third . . . that's a fancy name. You rich?"

A pleasant looking blond in green scrubs stood in the doorway, leaning on the handle of her mop.

"Sure," I said dryly. "Why not."

She smiled and peeked back out into the hallway. "I'm supposed to say 'Housekeeping.'"

"If I have my own housekeeper, I must be rich." I waved her in. "Feel free to keep house."

She moved easily about my hospital room, beautiful, effortless. She smelled good and paused often, most disconcerting. I felt her presence—not intense or weighty like Stormi's, but light, light and free, like so much fluff. It would be lying to say that scrub had no effect on me.

"I'm going to ask." She eased nearer the bed. "Why are you here? You don't look like the ones I usually see."

"How are we different?"

She quickly moved toward the door, shut it, and leaned her back against it before hurrying to my side. I instinctively made room on the bed and she plunked down.

"Well, for one thing, they don't have this."

And here she stretched out her hand and worked it through my blond hair. Honest. She touched me.

"And they sure don't have these." Her hand slipped down, stroking the contour of my shoulder, pausing on my bicep. "You're not hospital-typical."

"I'm not sick. But I'm here."

"You are."

At this point, I forgot my personality. Blame it on the fear of death. "Would you mind if I took your picture?"

"Go ahead. Wait, with that?"

"Yeah." I raised my 35mm to my eye. "Much better than a phone selfie."

What started as a dying man's last request morphed into an entire photo shoot. She posed, in ways both tempting and uncomfortable. After thirty shots, I let the camera fall to my side and leaned back.

"So, you're not sick." She tapped my forearm with her finger. "What are you, contagious?"

"Not contagious. Twisted."

The scrub smiled slyly, leaning over me. "I don't know if that's all bad."

"No, that's not, I'm actually—"

"Ahem."

The door was open, and Dad marched in.

I shifted, pushing myself higher. "Dad, meet . . ." I winced at my new friend.

"Hannah."

"Yes, Hannah. She's . . . well, she's apparently part of my spontaneous treatment plan. An important part, actually."

"Hmm," Dad said. "She looks to be at that."

I placed my hand on Hannah's. "Thank you for the encouragement. It was . . . encouraging."

Hannah's eyes twinkled. "You are most welcome, Jonah Everett the third."

She left and I fiddled with my shark tooth necklace, racked with guilt, as if I had gone behind Stormi's back. Feeling wanted is a powerful thing.

That evening, hours before the knife, I met with a bunch of other pre-surgical teens also in the final stages of their treatment plans.

Eight self-absorbed patients filed into a room and sat down in plush chairs to discuss the "emotions of the moment" and to celebrate our "oneness and inner wholeness." To everyone's credit, nobody said a darn thing for the longest time. With no facilitator, we sat there completely alone, and I thought that maybe this part of the treatment plan would work, since I could use a little peace.

My mind circled Stormi, remembered her leaning on my shoulder, and wished she were here. I replayed our last conversation. She'd never been wrong until now. Surgery definitely qualified as a procedure, and my wristband screamed full steam ahead.

I glanced around the circle, wondering if the other kids had their own Stormis, because none of them seemed present in the room. There were no jokes, and in the silence, a strange weight fell. Yep, I decided, it was a good group, every last one. Strange how the real possibility of premature death improves manners.

"What are we doing here?" said the kid sitting across from me.

Turned out his name was Gabe, who, like most gathered, was an epileptic awaiting brain surgery. Their seizures grabbed them and flung them to the ground too, or so Dad had said.

"Shut up. I'm searching for inner wholeness." This from Francis, a pretty girl from the face up. Another warped cottonwood, she kept peeking at me—or, more accurately, at my feet, since that was the direction of her gaze. This I only caught in my periphery, as I couldn't bear the sight of her straight-on. It's tough to gaze at yourself.

"How's that wholeness working for you?" Gabe smirked.

Francis shrugged. "I think I found some in my shoulder. My left shoulder. That feels pretty good right now."

"Ankles," another boy blurted. "My ankles are golden."

"Solid elbows." I touched each one. "Left, right. Solid. They screw up my elbows tomorrow and there's gonna be a lawsuit."

Ankles held out his fist and we bumped. "Where you from, Elbows? That's some accent."

"Nowhere, Oklahoma. We don't have an accent."

Ankles laughed. "Fair."

"Talk about wholeness, I have the healthiest back in the room. Wow, does my back feel good!" the nerdy guy with frames the size of Dad's windshield blurted, and the room fell quiet. He glanced around, clueless. "What? It does." He turned toward me. "My back feels awesome—Oh crap."

All eyes shifted to Francis and me.

"Well, Mr. Gold-Medal Back, my *brain* never felt better." I risked a peek into Francis's eyes. "How 'bout yours?"

"Perfect."

I laughed and she laughed and everyone else laughed and a nurse walked into the room and we all stopped laughing.

She sat down, found her somber face, and quickly had the room properly depressed.

"My name is Nurse Kalan, and it would be understandable if you kids were a little bit afraid. Your surgeries are major; I won't lie to you."

Why not? Now would be a really good time to tell a whopper.

She continued, "This time is your time to come together. To share your hearts."

My heart was another piece of me that worked perfectly. There would be zero chance of me sharing. The others must have felt the same.

Except for Holly.

Quiet until now, she burst to the fore.

"I'm Holly"—we all knew this from the dumb *Hello* badge she alone was wearing—"and this will be my fifth brain surgery. I'm not scared because it's my fifth. My first was scary though. Really scary. During my last surgery, I made it to the anesthesia count of ninety-six. That's kind of the game, and if any of you beat me . . . Well, none of you will, because you'll be out at ninety-eight. The anesthesia is seriously weird. Between that and the narcs, most people conk out or say something stupid before they even get to the counting, but not me, not this time. I'm going to lie there and count backward and still be lying and counting when I hit ninety-five."

She glanced triumphantly around the circle as if she had discovered her purpose in life. Ankles stared at me, his eyebrows raised. I shook my head. There was a girl in our midst living to reach ninety-five. Well, backward.

Nurse Kalan glanced at me. "Jonah? I noticed your response as she shared. Care to share *your* thoughts?"

"About Holly? No. You know, I hope she makes it tomorrow. To ninety-five, I mean." Nobody spoke. They all kept waiting and waiting, and they were probably just thinking about my perfect elbows, and I shouldn't have felt compelled to say any more on the eve of a near-death experience, but their eyes wouldn't shut up, so I said it. I thought of Stormi's words and I said it.

"I don't want to die."

And like that, Gabe flung forward. He hit the ground with force, his eyes rolled back, and he started to seize. It was fish-floppin' something. Kate, seated on my right, must've felt an intense kinship with him, because she joined him in a communal jerk-and-writhe session on the floor.

Now, epilepsy is not contagious, but I tell you this spectacle shook me. Ankles and Francis and the nerdy guy, they all dropped to their knees. Were they helping? Was everyone taking the oneness thing to extremes and seizing? I closed my eyes and listened to Nurse Kalan call for calm. Her voice muddled, morphed into gibberish, and my fingers tingled. A metallic taste filled my mouth and a ringing strengthened inside my ears. I tried to stand, to flee, but my legs were no longer my own and I struck the ground, feeling nothing.

A felled cottonwood, having his first seizure.

When I came to, I was gowned and bedded. Dad stared down at me with venom, quickly lowered the rail, and began to dress me, groggy as I was, in my own clothes.

"We're leaving."

It was all he said to me; all he said to the nurses and the doctor who attempted to dissuade him.

Dad had come to get me fixed, and this place had not only stolen his money, it had doubled his troubles. Three days after Christmas, he led me out into the frozen Minnesota night, helped me into the truck, and the next day we were back in Gullary.

I had two more seizures on that ride home, and following the second, miles from the Oklahoma border, I thought to tell him of Stormi's words. But it was too late. I'd already paid the price of ignoring her prediction.

Ma greeted us at the door, frowned at my back, and drew me close. "I'm not sure I understand."

"Doctors," Dad hissed, flinging his keys onto the table and vanishing into the back room.

I stood in front of my mother, watching her cry. I tried to straighten, but it hurt and I wasn't sure that it mattered anymore.

"I'm a monster," I said quietly. "Stormi won't want anything to do with me."

"Oh, honey, you're the most peaceful child I know."

"Wait," I whispered. "You haven't seen the nightmare."

Stormi shook me back to the present. "Off the path, Jonah. Quickly."

We crunched into the forest of hickory and oak and crouched behind a fallen log.

"I liked it *there*. Why are we here?" I whispered.

She shook her head, and I rolled my eyes.

Five minutes. Ten minutes. Then voices. Deep and hushed, men's voices joined the symphony of frogs and crickets from down the trail. The trudging of feet crackled the bracken, approaching, walking back toward Gullary.

Sun gave way to moon, and night shadow stole their faces from me, but it didn't matter; I knew these voices well.

"You know my stance on the matter. He doesn't need to be stayin' in Gullary no longer." Mr. Cartwright. "Nothing he said would hold weight."

"He does no harm inside. Can't be sure of anything if we let him out." Dad. *Dad?*

He continued. "Haste never provided us any benefit. It's why the mess started in the first place." Their feet paused on the holy ground where I'd held Stormi, and then three more men gathered. "I don't hear from Jonah that Tres is complaining. I say if it ain't broke—"

"And Stormi. What of her?" Men murmured and Cartwright's voice lowered. "My Gina says she's unnatural."

"Do we have a law against that?" Dad asked. "What would you have me do?"

"Many things can be done. Have been done." Mr. Cartwright pulled Dad nearer. "Shoot, I know Jonah's taken a likin' to her. And heaven knows that boy deserves some good his way. I'm startin' to think he's the reason you don't act."

Dad grabbed Cartwright by the shoulders. "I don't act because Stormi's done nothing wrong. Unexplained intuition is no reason for concern. You're on a witch hunt, and, David, I know why. It hurts. But what's done is done. We can't go back."

"Dang you, acting all innocent, Mr. Mayor! You've got chat under your fingernails like the rest of us." Cartwright shoved Dad, and then along with Mr. Tennyson pounded away across the moss bridge over the Green.

Dad swiped his hand over his head. "Men, this is going to get worse before it gets better. But the Circle must stay united. You understand the importance of this?"

Murmurs and nods, and together, three men plodded into the night.

Stormi took a deep breath. "Now would be another really good time to hold me."

I did, and she squeezed my arms tightly around her. What struck me as odd must've sounded a deeper chord in Stormi. An hour of mosquito-slapping minutes passed before she finally broke free. "It's safe now."

"What were they talking about? Unnatural? You haven't committed any crimes." I forced a chuckle, and my face hardened. "Have you?"

Stormi looked at me with those piercing browns; it was a sad look, both hopeful and resigned. The same look I got from Ms. Aldermaky when I failed trigonometry.

"Not yet."

"Not yet?"

She took my hand and pulled me back onto the path. I thought about that answer clear back to Gullary.

Stars appeared in the east, while the sun gave up one last streak of gray across the western sky. The lone cloud hovering above the hills caught the glint and whispered pink around its edges—a lot of beauty floated over our angry town.

"And why were they talking about Tres?" I asked. "Do you know about that?"

She hugged me and whispered, "Thank you for my birthday wish."

Birthday. Oh, birthday!

"Stormi, I have questions about what I heard, but I'm setting those down for now."

"Thank you."

"Yeah, no problem." I squinted, and rocked. The lie I was aiming to tell and the gift I was thinking to give were both out of character. "I'll be straight with you. I wasn't certain when your birthday was coming—we never knew before—but I thought I better be ready."

I dug in my pocket and pulled out the necklace. "It's real gold, I think. I thought it would look pretty on you, if you want it. I mean, I want you to want it—the necklace, that is. Oh, here."

I dropped the necklace into her hand, and she examined it for a long time, her face unreadable. Finally, she nodded. "Yeah, this is right." Then she exhaled, long and slow. "Put it on me, would you?"

"Sure." I fumbled with the clasp and her hair and the feel of her neck, but in time, I achieved my goal. "I think it's really good on you."

Stormi stroked it and stared toward SMX. "I'm scared, Jonah. It's like this whole town is holding its breath. A storm's coming, but I can't see it. Why can't I see it?"

"A storm? A funnel?"

Stormi winced. "I think worse. See you Monday morning, Jonah." She jogged away toward our trailer park.

I kicked at the dirt, experiencing none of Stormi's usual afterglow. In its place was dread, an anxious claw that ripped at my thoughts.

Cartwright. Dad. Stormi.

Not yet . . .

Worse?

CHAPTER 4

Sunday was dark.

Dark clouds billowed overhead. Dark questions ran through my mind.

It was dark with the memory of Dad and Mr. Cartwright in heated debate. Mr. Cartwright was a "bag o' wind," even Ma broke Christian charity to say so. But the fact that I had been involved in the debate sat sour with me, as did his flimsy concern for my well-being, which could blanket the truth no more than plastic wrap over a pig.

Mostly, Sunday felt empty because I didn't see Stormi.

I spent a fair piece of the morning gazing alternately at the hundred-plus photos of Stormi plastered on my walls and out my bedroom window at the Pickerings' trailer. As self-absorbed as I admittedly was, I worried all the more about Stormi in that double-wide. This because Connor lived there, and where I had trouble speaking clearly when Stormi was near, Connor expressed his perverse passions with ease.

He wasn't safe. I told Stormi as much.

"I know," was all she'd say.

So, on days when Ms. P had the 5 a.m. at Sophie's Diner, I watched, knowing nothing but Stormi's knack for the prophetic would keep her from harm's way.

"Sorry, Mr. E!"

Connor's voice cut through the open window, and I frowned and scampered to the front of our trailer. I cracked the blinds.

There was Dad, tossing a baseball to Connor.

I loved baseball.

They stood thirty feet apart, nodding and firing. Nodding and firing. Their gloves swallowed each ball with a thwack. I tried to leave, but I couldn't pull free from that stupid window.

Couldn't take my eyes off my happy dad. My happy, talkative dad.

"You've got a good arm, Connor. You're a strong kid— young man, I should say."

Thwack.

"You know, son, I forget how much I miss this."

Son?

Thwack. I heard Connor's throw strike Dad's glove. *Thwack.* And I felt Dad's words nail my gut. *Thwack.* And I thought to dig for my mitt and join them, to show them I could play. That I was worth playing with. That I wasn't some cripple.

"You know, son, I'm heading out fishing tomorrow." Dad gestured toward our trailer with his head. "Can't really risk him on open water. Have any interest?"

Thwack.

I retreated from the glass, the sound of the ball and Dad's words tossing about in my brain. *So, Dad, you found a replacement.*

I hauled my defective self back to my bedroom. Ten minutes later, a knock at the door. I made no move to answer.

Dad peeked in. "How long are you planning on eyeing our neighbors?" He plunked beside me on the bed, mitt still on his hand.

I boiled. Even before I saw him with Connor, Dad had that effect. All my classmates had long ago snipped their umbilicals, but not me. Not with the seizures. Without a driver's license, I needed Dad to shuttle me, Ma to buy my medicine, both of them to speak gently when Ol' Rick took me at home. Yeah, I needed them—hated needing them. I found rage much easier to bear than shame.

"You know . . ." Dad leaned into my shoulder—granted a fatherly gesture, but I was simmering and muscled his weight off me. "We live too close for you to ogle the day away. That type of surveillance isn't healthy." He glanced at my photos, the ones that captured every nuance of her. That's what I was, a nuance collector.

"Not sure your obsession with her is healthy either."

"Neither is *Connor's*, your baseball buddy. And you know his sick thoughts," I hissed.

Dad gently set his mitt on the floor and folded his hands. Two minutes passed. Then five. I peeked over at the man. He exhaled slow and loud, and then tousled my hair.

It takes a fair piece of energy to hate a person for any length of time. Maybe if this had been the first time I'd seen them together, I could have stoked the fire, but it wasn't and I calmed.

With the anger went my wonderings about the secrecy and mystery of the night before. I was with Dad. A jerk sometimes, yeah, but as decent a dad as could be found in Gullary.

I tracked a silhouette, followed closely by a larger shadow, moving behind the Pickerings' kitchen shade.

"Oh, I know Connor's a scoundrel." Dad chuckled and lowered his head. "I see it each time he mocks you. And believe you me, if I hear of that young man causing trouble in there, I will . . . well, I'll force the Circle to move its hand. How's that?"

The Circle. Five men with the authority to pass judgment on the citizens of Gullary. My father was the unpaid mayor, but it was his position in the Circle that gave him power.

Dad often told the story of an out-of-control former mining town and Granddad's solution. A Circle with the town's blessing to act as judge and jury. With the SMX at their disposal, there was no need to involve the courts or outsiders. Gullary could take care of its own problems.

The Circle, accountable to no one, was effective, and soon there was no crime in Gullary, a source of pride even today. Gullary still did not employ a single police officer.

Dad's arm rounded my shoulder, tried to straighten my spine. "But I don't think we'll need to get involved. Time's on Stormi's side. The two of you are weeks from setting school behind you. I don't figure she'll stick around our quiet town after graduation." He paused. "Do you?"

The room was silent. A little too much so.

"What's wrong with Gullary?"

"Oh, nothing. I'm not saying that. It just seems like a young lady with so much going for her wouldn't find much purpose here." He gave my chest a thump. "Best let her go now. People like Stormi have a bigger place in the world. You'd do her a favor to tell her that."

Bigger place than me, huh?

"Why do you think she landed here?" I asked.

"Ma would say Providence, but there are other forces at work in this world."

I rubbed my face, frowned. "Like what?"

"Oh, painful forces without names. But they come without warning. There are times when life is going well, when you're headed in a wonderful . . ."

"Trajectory?"

"Exactly right, Jonah. A wonderful trajectory. And from out of nowhere, the unbelievable happens, and all you love gets turned upside down. You keep breathing. That's all you can do." His voice trailed off. "Keep breathing."

I felt certain that one of Dad's unnamed forces, thick and weighty, had settled in my bedroom.

"Now come on." He forced a smile, and gently backhanded my shoulder. "Mom'll be back from church soon, and I promised her the place would be spotless. That's a two-man job."

Spring cleaning took the rest of the day, but I glanced through the curtain each time I strode by the window. Someday Stormi would need me like I needed her, and, once again, Aragorn would be there.

CHAPTER 5

If Sunday was dark, Monday was flat-out inky.

Rain fell in sheets, and I splashed through mud puddles, bounding up the Pickerings' steps. I raised my hand to knock, but never struck wood. Stormi burst out, slamming the door behind her.

"What's going on?" My, but she was shaking.

"Do you think your dad, your mom, might take me in?"

I squinted. "What's he doing to you?"

"Do you think they'd take me in now?"

"Ma took in that stray German shepherd last year, so I don't see her objecting. Dad would be tougher, but if there was a reason." I paused. "You have to tell me. Is there a reason?"

Stormi gathered herself straight, offering a mighty body shake. Then composure returned.

"Well, let's give it some thought. Connor isn't bearable any longer." Stormi reached out her hand, and let the rain splash against her palm. "Beautiful day." She squeezed my forearm. "Get me away from here."

Again, the door flew open.

Connor stared at Stormi. Of all the emotions a soul can string together, contempt and want are the most terrifying. I tell you, that is what I saw. He turned those eyes toward me, and good old-fashioned disgust took over. "So, Stormi, we're done, huh?" An evil heart says those words while looking at another. "That was all?"

"We never started. We never will." Stormi's hand worked its way into mine, and Connor's jaw tightened.

"Hey, Fish. No flopping yet, huh? Well, the day's young."

"I, I don't—"

I never stuttered, unless I was near a Pickering. Stormi, out of adoration. Connor, from sheer hatred.

"What's that?" Connor leaned forward, bent down. "I missed what you said. Were you talking to me or the ground?"

My mouth opened, shut, and I shook my head. Connor was twenty-one. Connor was an idiot. He had no job, unless alcohol consumption could be considered an occupation. But Connor had good looks on his side, and in Gullary that stood for something. I'd seen most every girl in town climb into his truck. Except for one. The one he couldn't have.

The one I knew he wanted most of all.

Connor reached for Stormi's arm and she recoiled.

"Easy, sis. Why don't I drive you to school? Heck, Hunchie can come too. We'll throw the beast in back."

Stormi spun me around and ducked under my umbrella. "Let's go."

We left slowly beneath the pattering of raindrops and the occasional peal of thunder, and though Stormi relaxed, I admit the exchange had wounded me. Those for whom you have no regard shouldn't know the ways to skewer your heart, but with a word, Connor Pickering could leech blood like no other.

"Finals today." Stormi broke the silence. "World History and Psych. Should be passable."

"For you." I glanced over and noticed that she still wore the necklace, the one I gave her. "Hey, you're wearing the—"

"Connor saw it and went a little crazy. He guessed who it came from." She touched it gently. "I think this gift might cause both of us some problems. Do you want me to lose it?"

"It's not the necklace he hates. It's the you-and-me, right?"

She said nothing.

"And I can't lose that."

Stormi leaned her head on my shoulder. "He can't figure us out."

"Nobody can." I paused. "Neither can I. Everyone stares at perfect you—"

"Not perfect."

"And then they look at *Deformicus flopicus fishicus*—"

"I hate when you do that stupid Latin thing."

"Point is," I said, "you can obviously spend your time with anyone you want and you pretty much hang with me. Someday, possibly, you'll tell me why?"

Maybe I didn't raise my tone at the end of that sentence. Or maybe she didn't hear me beneath the splat of raindrops overhead. Either way, she left my question dangling unanswered. "You know," she straightened, "we're a little early to head to the bus stop. Let's take the long way, around the chat pile."

I shrugged, and we huddled and walked, listening to the pound of straight-down rain bouncing off the umbrella.

We reached the first heap and Stormi grabbed my hand. "Hold up here."

She stared at that pile, ten stories tall and mixed with fine tailings. When it rained, those tailings traced grooved streams down the mound.

Stormi peeked down at her feet, at the toxic pool forming around us.

The slop filled my shoes. "You, uh, you want to keep standing in a poisonous pond?"

She shushed me with her finger and kept staring at the ground.

She's unnatural.

The words popped in, and I pushed them out. Unusual, maybe, but not unnatural.

"Do you ever feel there's something you should be doing?" Stormi stared straight ahead. "Something important? Do you ever feel like you're wandering through life, walking in circles, running from something, when right in front of you is this big thing?"

"Like a chat pile?"

She glared.

"Sorry," I said. "No, I, uh, I don't. But you'll figure it out. You always do. Even Dad thinks so. He says you're about to leave." I hadn't planned on bringing Dad into this, but he sort of fit. "Are you, you know, leaving Gullary?"

"Yes."

I kid you not; right here a rumble of thunder shook the sky.

What do you do when half of your heart sprouts legs and decides to walk out the door? How does half a person live?

"Where you going? Is it far?"

"From you? Not so far." She stepped out of the sludge and shook her feet. "It's time. We better get to the stop."

We walked to Washington Ave. and swung onto 2nd Street. In the distance, the bus stop was alive with drippy laughter. A puddle fight beneath a lightning storm. The senior class was soaked, except for Gina and Yolanda, who stood on the far side of the street.

Such was school for seniors in May. It kicked the maturity level back a few years. Which probably explained the rash of parking lot vandalism at school the previous week. Which absolutely explained the principal banning all students from driving to finals. Which unfortunately meant a special, early bus had to be sent to Gullary solely for the senior class.

Which was the reason for the impromptu water fight happening at the bus stop.

We eased up, and Stormi squeezed my forearm. "I no longer need the umbrella, Jonah."

I frowned and stepped away, still thinking about her departure. Rain fell hard on Stormi's upturned face, and she closed her eyes. She always said she listened better beneath clouds, and if true, whatever she heard today would fall loud and clear.

The bus to Waxton-Gullary Senior High hydroplaned to a stop in front of us, sending a swath of water onto jeans and bare legs, but nobody cared.

Especially Stormi.

We boarded, all except for my friend, who stood as a statue, palms raised, jaw set.

Unnatural.

Hank, the bus driver and a stickler for time, offered two honks. Late to school was forgivable. Late for finals, a different matter.

"Commune with the world after you graduate!" Hank held a newspaper above his head and poked his baldness out the bus door. "I give you ten seconds and then I'm leavin' without you."

She didn't move.

"Stormi!" I hollered out the window. "Come on!"

Hank turned to me. "Sorry, Jonah. Whatever's gotten ahold of her can't throw me off schedule."

I sighed, the brakes hissed.

And Stormi jumped in front of the bus.

"Whoa!" Bus brakes squealed.

Stormi leaped around and slapped the accordion door, which quickly opened. Chuckles faded to strange silence. Stormi hopped up, scanned our faces, and rubbed her own.

"All of you, off the bus," she whispered. Her breath was heavy, and she grabbed my arm, her voice gaining strength. "Off the bus! Everyone!"

"That girl needs medical attention." Hank levered the door shut and pulled out. "Enough theater. Sit down."

Stormi stared at me, wild-eyed. I knew what she was asking.

Right now, I'd sure appreciate a normal best friend.

I took a deep breath and walked up the aisle. "No, Hank." I jammed my foot on the brake, and again we screeched to a stop.

"Foot. Off. My bus." Hank reached down and lifted my leg.

"Why not open up? Give the kids who want to get off the chance."

He squinted, massaging his temple. "You're letting affection warp good sense. Mayor's going to hear of this."

"I know. Believe me, I know."

Hank smirked and opened the door. "Well, I remember a time when I would've done the same for a girl. Been a few years now."

Stormi quickly walked down the aisle, touching the shoulder of every classmate except for Gina, who swatted her with a math textbook. When she again reached the front of the bus, her voice was calm and settled and held more authority than I thought possible.

"I will tell you one last time." She pointed at the door. "Get off this bus."

Her eyes turned terrible, so terrible that I almost didn't recognize her. So terrible that seventeen kids risked failing finals and stepped into the rain. When finally the bus did pull out, only one face remained pressed against the glass. Gina Cartwright.

It was the last time I ever saw her.

"Cat Jones had a view of the whole thing." My legs felt weak, and I slumped down against the cell opposite Tres's. "You know the pole bridge over Limon River? How that turn onto it comes out of the blue? Well, due to the rain, Cat was shutting down his irrigation, and our bus came screaming by fast. Way too fast, given conditions. Cat jumped the fence and stepped onto Washout Road in time to see the bus squeal, misjudge the right, crash straight through the old fence, and drop from view. Cat hauled after it and peeked down into the river. The bus landed on its head. Hank, Gina, they didn't live."

Tres stared at his dinner tray.

"Only one kid on that bus?" His voice sounded far away. "That was a stroke of fortune."

I shook my head and tapped the floor slow and rhythmic. "That was the unnatural part."

Tres's gaze shot up. "Some got off before, didn't they?"

"Some."

"And it was Stormi." He whispered, "She knew."

"I can't find her. Haven't seen her since. The rest of us got off that bus and drifted back into town. But not Stormi. She wandered after the bus, crying, I think. Stormi never cries." I sighed hard and pointed at his tray. "If it wasn't for her, there'd be no chili in your cell."

Tres stood and paced. "There shouldn't be chili in this cell," he muttered. "That crash finally would've ended it." He pounded the wall.

"Ended what? My life? Yeah, it would have. It would have wiped the senior class of Gullary off the face of this earth. And you seem to be taking the accident's side." I stared at Tres. Maybe he'd been locked up so long, he misunderstood key portions of my narrative, but I still thought seeing me alive would provide him a little happiness. "It's strange. Walking around today. Coming here today. It feels almost wrong."

Tres sighed. "Here." He shoved Ma's cooking back into the hall. "I ain't hungry no more, and you deserve a good meal. You were on death row, all right, and Stormi done issued a last-second pardon."

Tres opened his drawer and pulled out a sheet of paper, ripped it in two, and scribbled a quick note. He glanced at the rip, shaved little bits off the torn edge, and held it up to the light. "Close enough. For you. Pocket it and set your eyes on it later. After things calm down 'round here."

I rose and nodded, took the note, and trudged slowly toward the red door.

"Hey, Jonah!"

I stopped but did not turn. "Yeah."

"I am mighty glad you got off the bus."

I closed the red door behind me and glanced around the gallery. Another ripped note, this one from Stormi, rested on the counter.

Need to get away for a few days.
Please, come see me.

Take the birthday path to our place.

I lumbered home and into my room, where I began a frantic stuffing. Extra clothes, wool hat, and a flashlight all went into my pack. Who knew how long we'd stay?

"Jonah."

I spun around. Dad and Ma stood in the doorway, their faces somber.

"Where is she?" Dad asked.

"She? Can you be a bit more specific?"

"Jonah, not the time for that."

"Kinda is. Stormi, then?"

Ma walked in, glanced at my pack, and sat on my bed. "There are some questions that beg answers. And right now, I think she is the only one who has them."

"I don't follow."

Ma started to speak, but Dad shushed her and took a step forward. "David Cartwright lost his daughter in a bus accident that, by all accounts, Stormi had foreknowledge of." He glanced at her photos covering my wall and stuffed his hands in his pockets. "This is no small thing. How did she know? Unless she knew who meddled with the brakes, Jonah, she could not. We both know she lives in an . . . unstable environment."

"Brakes fail. By themselves. No meddling required. And buses lose control in storms. This isn't the first time she's predicted a tragedy." I paused. "Wait, you said 'unstable environment.' You're saying Connor did it."

"More likely—and don't take this wrong—it was Stormi herself. Greasy Jake confirmed that she worked on that bus in his shop not more than a week ago. Mr. Cartwright is convinced she's the one."

Of all the stupid sentences my dad had strung together over the years, these were so far afield I could hardly speak.

I straightened as much as I could and walked toward my father. "You should be thankful for what she did this morning. She saved the entire class. She saved me."

He winced, and I wanted to smack him.

"Speaking of you, son, from your classmates' reports, it sounds like you had a hand in the proceedings as well."

"Well, yeah, I stopped the bus by stomping on perfectly good brakes. Can we agree that's a good thing?"

"I think what your father is trying to say is that he needs to know who knew what, and how they knew it." Ma sighed. "Please, where is she, Jonah?"

I peered around my room, thinking on what to share, what to hold. "I'm going to see her now, and in a few days we'll come back. And when we do, you can talk to her." I lowered my voice. "Stormi's done nothing wrong. Unexplained intuition is no reason for concern." I peeked into Dad's eyes. "Isn't that how it went?"

Dad glanced sharply. "Yeah. That's how it went." He folded his arms, and the muscles in his jaw tensed and then loosened. "If you can convince me that your return will be imminent."

I dug in my pocket and yanked out a note. "Doesn't sound like I can convince you of anything, but . . ." I unfolded the sheet and flattened it over my knee. It wasn't Stormi's handwriting. "Oh, wrong note." Stormi's came out next, and I laid it on my desk.

Dad read the words. "Her birthday? I didn't know."

"Neither did I."

He pushed his hand through his hair. "All right. I'll appease David. I trust a private message from Stormi to you reveals her plans. But you may not leave before the funeral. All the Everetts will pay their respects to Gina. It's only right. Stormi can wait."

I stared at my pack. "But I can't contact her. There's no reception at the . . . You know what? Fine. Deal."

"Deal." Dad exhaled hard. "Now can I see the other note?"

"It's not from her," I said.

Dad raised his eyebrows.

"What?" I frowned. "It's not!"

He reached out his hand.

"I'm an adult. You can look at it, but next time trust me a little. I haven't read it yet myself." I threw it in his direction.

Dad bent over, scooped it up, and placed the sheet below Stormi's. "Deceit helps nobody, Jonah. Has she given you still more?" He tongued his cheek.

I walked to the desk, reached down and flattened the pieces of paper. The tear lined up perfectly. It was more than the same note; it was the same sheet. Given to me by two different people.

"But that can't be." I leaned over the words. "How did Tres get the other half? I saw him rip it and write it. And she won't go near him."

"Tres. You got the bottom lines from Tres?" Dad glanced at Ma and then back to me. "Did you tell him what happened?"

"Not that specific detail. He couldn't have known the number."

Dad spun and strode out of the room. Ma placed a trembling hand over her mouth, stroked my head, and then followed him out.

I blinked and reread the entire note.

> Need to get away for a few days.
> Please, come see me.
>
> Take my birthday path to our place.
>
> I should never have saved any of those
> eighteen kids.
>
> It would have been a fair trade.
>
> I didn't do my job, and that's because
> of Jonah.

CHAPTER 6

I woke early to the crisp lightness of a blue sky, a hinting at the clear day to come. But it did not feel clear. I grabbed my camera, hoping to take some shots, eager to find beauty through my lens and return to normal. But as I stepped out the trailer door, the weight of some unnatural fog settled over me. It turned out that I wasn't the only one.

Confusion surrounding the accident drew Gullary's students together.

Signs and banners sprung up outside houses, on storefronts.

WE ARE GULLARY

REMEMBER GINA

Truth be told, nobody cared much for Gina while she drew breath, and it pains me now even to mention it. Death muddies the realities of life. Unexplainable words began to circulate about her final moments on this earth, words recounting heroic actions and steadfast convictions. Had she not remained resolute, while the rest of us fled the doomed bus? Like a captain, sacrificing her life as her crew escaped on lifeboats, wasn't that Gina?

The high school called it quits three days early in light of events; final exams were administered via the postal service.

That day before the funeral, I saw all but two of my classmates: Gina and Stormi.

The senior class floated aimlessly through town in small patches beneath that cloudless sky. What were we doing? Why were we wandering? I can't say, except that whenever I saw one of the fortunate ones who exited the bus, I knew they felt as I did.

We were the walking dead. Those who should not be alive. Mortality had come to Gullary in search of victims and, finding only two, decided to take up residence. It clouded my thoughts, troubled my dreams. None of us knew how to handle it.

Least of all me.

I couldn't stay inside the museum, and after making a silent six a.m. food delivery to a sleeping Tres, I locked the gallery and shuffled through town, hoping to meet my classmates. Usually my mockers and tormenters, the sight of them held no dread; without Stormi to make sense of my feelings, isolation was my only enemy.

Strange. One life ends and the living cling to each other all the more.

Wally, six foot seven and the closest thing Gullary had to an athlete, hailed me from behind while I meandered down Main Street.

I stopped, and he jogged up to me. "Jonah, I, uh, thanks, man. Yeah, that's it. No, thank her too."

I couldn't remember the last time Wally had spoken to me. It felt good, and for an instant, I mattered. Had I not been the one to slam the brakes? To plead our case before Hank, and save everyone but Gina? But pride is fleeting, especially when unjustified. It had been Stormi, and Stormi alone. Had I been alone, we'd all be dead.

"I'll tell her, if I see her." I glanced over his shoulder. Carly and Madison fast approached, their faces puffy and red.

A word on Carly and Madison: They existed at the top of the food chain. Girls, Stormi excluded, fought and scratched for the pair's approval. Guys seeking bragging rights hungered for more than that.

Both gave Wally a hug, long and real, and then turned to me. Awkward moments ensued.

"Can't stay inside today," Carly finally said, rubbing her eyes with the heel of her hand. "It's so totally depressing. It's like suffocating or something." She paused. "I mean, what if I would've stayed on the bus? I could've sat there. There was no reason to get out. It was raining and we had finals. How did you and Stormi know that would happen?" she asked, but did not wait for my reply. "I mean, I know she knows things."

"I didn't have a clue—"

"It doesn't matter. I'm not believing Dad. Stormi wouldn't do that to Gina, and she warned her too. It's so weird today." She scuffed the sidewalk with her sandal. "We're still alive, right?"

In that instant, Carly passed from know-nothing to deep thinker, at least in my book. She nailed it, the question we were all asking, and the reason we were walking the streets.

We wanted to feel the warmth, the breeze. We needed reassurance our feet still touched the earth.

Carly gave me a hug. Maybe it wasn't as long as the one Wally received, but it counted nonetheless. Madison, two notches harsher but five notches more attractive, followed suit.

A stranger to appreciation, I found it as awkward as a group shower in phys ed, and stuttered some drivel about thanking Stormi when I see her and feeling in shock and wishing Gina was still here.

The mention of Gina's name extracted a fresh round of tears from the girls, which was followed by more hugs for me.

My presence had a very different effect on adults. Even those whose kids Stormi had saved cast wary glances my way. I had become an Other, like Stormi. Suspect. No longer homegrown Jonah with an unfortunate back and brain. No longer one to pity.

One who left Gina to die. One who could have done more. One to dread.

My wanderings carried me into the DairyWhip, one of the few open businesses, and I plunked down my dollar.

Mrs. Contulky emerged quickly from the back, drying her hands on her apron. "What can I get for—" Our gazes locked, and I offered my most pleasant smile. Her face pruned, and she slowed and swallowed hard, her lower lip pinched between her teeth. "Can I help you?"

I frowned and lowered myself onto a stool. "Well, yeah. It's me, Jonah? Same as always. Cone. Vanilla. A little caramel?" I cast her a sideways glance. "Please?"

She peered at me a moment before slowly reaching for the bill and turning toward the soft-serve machine.

"People treat you strangely." This from Arthur, sitting at the far end of the counter. "That was an eleven-second stare she gave you. Your regular order has never garnered you an eleven-second stare."

He hopped up and hunkered down next to me. Arthur Bales was the one person I did not want to see today.

A senior like myself, he had also been on the bus, but not even death could faze Arthur. Was he happy? Was he distraught? His face offered no tells. Of all the students in Gullary, he alone, as far as I could recollect, had never mocked me. Maybe because hiding behind the largest glasses in town was a kid who had taken his own lumps. Or perhaps his eyesight was so poor, he simply hadn't noticed my hunch.

Arthur was odd, his affect rarely matching the moment. Socially, he was lost in this world. But he was brilliant, claiming to have an IQ of 160 or some number in the stratosphere. Still, he failed English Lit and Chemistry and Health, instead choosing to master all of life's minute details, which pretty much made his IQ irrelevant.

"Hey, Arthur. Some day, huh?" I stared straight ahead and reached out for my cone. Mrs. Contulky set it down on the counter and walked quickly into the back room.

"It's a beautiful morning." Arthur took one last slurp of Cherry Freezie. "Where's Stormi?"

"I'm not exactly sure," I lied.

Arthur nodded, reached for a pepper shaker, and slid it across the counter until it rested between us. He squinted at that shaker, and finally nodded. "I've been thinking about this for some time now. I have decided on my next move."

"What next move? Oh no. Your little chess match will need to wait. I fed Tres this morning and I'm not going back to see him for a while."

"I need you to make the move." Arthur started a nervous tap on the counter. "I need it done today."

"No."

Arthur shook, as was his custom when presented with a curveball. "Bishop to G5," and then louder, "Bishop to G5. Zugzwang. Yet again, he's done it to me. The evils of zugzwang."

"Zig—"

"Zugzwang! He forces me to make a move, but every move weakens my position. This man is an expert at placing me in zugzwang." Arthur leaned over. "Are you sure I'm not battling a computer?"

I laughed. "No. I wish you could see the man you're playing. Imagine a severely tooth-deficient old guy. But our agreement needs to hold. Tres can't communicate with the outside world. You're playing completely under the table. No mentioning him except to me."

"I haven't been illegal!" He pounded the counter. "Move me! Zugzwang. Zugzwang!"

I glanced at Arthur, picked up the shaker, and sighed. How strange our minds were. His brain was brilliant, but he couldn't handle the slightest change of plans. My brain, completely unbrilliant, yet it hurtled me to the floor whenever it chose.

"I tell you what. After tomorrow's funeral . . ." I took a slurp of melting ice cream. "I'll head over and see Tres. There's an unusual note issue we need to discuss, and I'll inform him of your move then."

Arthur's eyes glazed. He seemed to retreat deep inside himself, to a lonely land I didn't want to visit. His eyebrows furrowed and his lips tensed. He shook free and quick glanced my way. "Yes. That will be fine." I smiled and patted his straight back. On a day filled with confusion, the predictably quirky behavior of Arthur calmed me.

I glanced at my cone. It was no longer appealing, and I pushed off the stool and tossed it into the garbage.

"Have a good day, Arthur. And you too, Mrs. Contulky!"

No response from the back, but as I exited the door, Arthur called, "Remember the move. Bishop to G5."

I stepped into daylight with Arthur's words on my mind. He wasn't the only one in zugzwang. Me, Stormi; it seemed like every move we made angered somebody. Dad, Ma, Mr. Cartwright . . . somebody. I couldn't wait to see my beautiful friend, but already I feared our eventual return home.

She'd be asked to explain how she knew, and she'd give the answer she always gave, the one that was frustrating and evasive, and never satisfied: "The truth unfolds. It just unfolds a little faster for me than it does for you."

Zugzwang.

I spotted the perfect kicking stone on Main Street. It was red limestone and the size of a golf ball and it stayed with me all the way home to A Street, where I gave it one last kick toward our trailer. It bounced off the gravel street, and skipped across the grass that long ago took over the driveway. It came to rest beneath our lean-to, beneath the lawn tractor.

My blasted lawn tractor.

Trucks were the standard set of wheels for teens in Gullary. Not for an epileptic. As a seizure-free year seemed an impossibility, Dad downgraded expectations and traded five chickens for an orange Husqvarna riding mower.

He washed it up, and, with great ceremony, walked me outside with his paw over my eyes.

"I bought you something. Every kid needs a set of wheels."

"You're kidding me!" In that moment, all Dad's faults were forgiven. "But I can't drive!"

He removed his hand, and rounded my shoulder with his arm. "Sure you can. You didn't think I'd be so cruel as to buy you something you can't use."

I stared at that stupid tractor.

No, I would never think you could be cruel.

"So, is something wrong with the push mower?" I asked.

He walked over and leaned against the Husky, kicked the tire. "You misunderstand. This is not for work, this is for your transportation. *This* is for pleasure."

"Pleasure."

"I'm not as old as you might think. I remember the free-dom a good set of wheels can bring."

I coughed. "So this is for dates, and road trips, and all that freedom stuff."

"Might take a few modifications, but this deck here, that'll support a bag of groceries, your meds." He walked back, a twinkle in his eye. "Can't say that this might not improve your prospects around here. Girls like a guy with his own wheels."

I knew he was trying—in his own way, he was trying—but I could not endure it.

"It's a flippin' mower! I can't drive this around Gullary. So, what, I go on a date, and five hours later we pull in to the Waxton drive-in, blades blazing? We make out, cut the lawn, make out some more?"

"Calm, son. It's for transportation, not procreation." His face fell. "Things are different now. You're different now. The quicker we accept that what you aren't . . . that you aren't . . . you know—"

"No, I don't. What am I not?"

He looked off. "Normal."

Dad left his abnormal son standing alone, staring at his ride. One week later, I drove my tractor to the drugstore. Two weeks later, Stormi removed the blade and replaced the engine. She turned it into a 40 mph machine, able to reach top in-town speeds.

But I never did take Stormi to the drive-in.

Only jerks could do that.

I turned my gaze from my tractor, and stared at our trailer. Silent. The hills swallowed all sound in Gullary, and with Stormi gone, it seemed quieter still.

The outside of our home was falling apart. Shingles hung crooked, and the screen door sported one hinge. Dad lacked the basic handyman skills common to most men in town. Even the mailbox stood cocked.

Mailbox. I wonder.

I walked toward the Pickerings' and peeked inside. One letter. Stamped and outbound.

A letter from Stormi.

Tampering with the mail was a big-deal offense, but every so often, generally late at night, I took the risk.

I removed the envelope and quick-stepped inside. I hurried into my room, plopped on the bed, and stared at the writing. They were always addressed the same.

Mom

1111 Wherever St.

Home, KS 51111

Kansas. Do you know that?

I slid my finger beneath the flap, and fell onto my back.

Dear Mom,

It was great to see you.

Eighteen, it was a really special birthday. Glad you took some time out from your busy life to come see me. I felt we shared some nice moments. Oh, you know, the moment we didn't have together watching the sunrise. Then there was that nice moment we didn't have hiking toward the Green. Oh, and then my candle moment; that was another nice birthday moment we didn't share.

Don't worry; Jonah took your place. Again. He always does. He always will. That's who he is—dependable, caring, concerned—all the things a mother should be.

Sorry. It's just that I really could use you right now. Right now I'm messing up in every way possible. Right now, Connor is out of control, and I won't give him any more space in this note. Right now, everyone in Gullary thinks I messed up by doing something good, and I'm starting to believe them.

But not Jonah. I keep coming back to him, but he keeps coming back for me. I can't lose him; he's all I have. I used to feel that way about you.

I wish you two could meet. He'd show you how a mother should be.

Your daughter,

Stormi

p.s. What did you name me?

I gently folded the note and opened my bed stand drawer, slipping it alongside ten other Stormi letters resting there. I pounded the wall, and enjoyed the throb in my hand.

Dependable, caring, and concerned. All the things a mother should be.

Again, I hit the wall, and felt a maternal ache.

CHAPTER 7

Two occasions typically animated the entire town of Gullary: funerals and the Fourth of July. This year, while one committee planned to celebrate the birth of our country, another, with equal fervor, planned to mourn the death of a girl. The irony was not lost on anyone, and the town was buzzing.

Yet something was lost: all talk of Hank the bus driver. For nearly forty years, he shuttled kids back and forth, safely running his daily routes. Three generations of residents had seen the inside of his bus. In life, he was an institution.

In death, an afterthought.

His quiet service in neighboring Waxton received little mention, even in the *Gazette*, the local paper quick to report every stubbed toe and skunk sighting. Gina's photos filled its pages, even warranting a special memorial issue to honor "Gullary's precious lost jewel." This attention, of course, was due to her young age and her father's status on the Circle.

Dad was right. What the Circle wanted, the Circle got.

But not Mr. Cartwright, not today, and it was easy to feel for the man.

Gullary squeezed into the Baptist church, which seemed to please Deacon Holmes.

"Welcome, welcome. So glad you're here." He worked the somber crowd in the foyer. "It's so nice to gather, isn't it?"

For all the homage paid to Gina, there had been no wake, no open casket—no chance to say good-bye. Mr. Cartwright had not allowed it. Instead, he requested that the entire senior class receive special seating in the front two pews.

Painfully hard, those forward pews. Pitched over in the packed second row, my bulging vertebrae knobbed against the straight oaken back. I scooted up an inch, giving in to my natural bend, and rested my forehead on the seat in front.

Directly behind me sat the Pickerings, minus Stormi, of course. Ms. P and Connor seemed amazingly at peace, given they had no clue where Stormi had gone. Then again, Ms. P gave up on parental involvement long ago. Connor was proof of that.

The church was thick and silent. The nasally organ that accompanied these affairs had also been nixed by Gina's father. There were no whispers. No crying. Just the occasional cough or creak of wood.

Mr. Cartwright seemed determined to put all of us through a near-death experience.

On the casket rested one yellow rose, and beside it, in front of the stage, a large framed photo of Gina from seventh grade. She was smiling, without a care, her braces glinting. Gina never looked that good in real life.

Mr. Cartwright strode before the rows of sardine-packed seniors. He looked at each one of us in turn. It was a fearsome gaze. A how-dare-you-be-alive gaze. He paused in front of me.

"We will have words following."

I peeked up and nodded, and he turned and took his place across the aisle.

A tap on my neck. "Man looks serious," Connor whispered. "Don't envy you, explaining to Cartwright why you and Stormi axed his daughter."

I spun around. "What the heck?"

"Shh!" Ma's hushing reached me from the back of the church. I rolled my eyes and reassumed my position.

Only stupid Connor. Let it go.

"Now would be a good time for one of those seizures. A real big one," Connor's whisper again floated to my ears. I swatted the air to quiet him, but he was determined to see my party trick.

"What comes first? Ma says its dizziness. Or is it tingling?" He leaned way forward. "Stormi says your vision blurs; yeah, in our moments she tells me everything." He ran his fingers across the hairs on my neck. "Are we tingling? Is it blurry yet?"

The power of suggestion is a mighty weapon, and Connor knew how to wield it. There, resting on the pew, I turned my head, and needles prickled my fingertips.

Not here.

Had I been at home, maybe it would have stopped there; maybe I could have ignored the sensation and my mind would have quieted.

But in the church, cramped, tense, and on display before the entire town, Old Rickety eased onto my lap.

I closed my eyes tight, and when next I opened them, Carly, seated to my right, was fuzzy, as if someone were taking a giant eraser to her edges. I blinked hard, and she doubled, not sideways but up. One Carly floated on top of another Carly.

Old Rickety reached inside.

My hand clawed, and Carly scooted away in horror. I quickly stood and stumbled over her legs, desperate to escape. I reckoned I had about twenty seconds to make it out of the church.

I reached only the aisle. I crashed to the floor, and there, for the next ten minutes, the entire town of Gullary witnessed my funeral, my little death. Only there was no casket in which to hide, and I didn't die. Not completely.

I remained partly conscious throughout my thrashing. Those were always the tough ones. Thrown about, while my mind suspended me in that middle place—like the murky end to a nightmare. Terror has you bound and you can't wake up.

My thoughts were still my own, and while on the floor they traveled from Connor to Gina to wondering how pissed Mr. Cartwright would be that I stole the show at his daughter's funeral. I wondered about my positioning, how visible my hunch was to the audience, had I struck oak on the way down, and if so, was my pressed white shirt now stained crimson.

I wondered why the God of this good universe took time to fashion a freak.

My body finally stilled and my vision stabilized.

Crap.

The easel and Gina's picture frame lay in splinters beneath me. There was Ma, crying softly at my side. Dad sat on the stage and gently cradled my head. I wished Stormi would appear, and on the heels of that hope, I wished I would vanish. But neither happened and there I was, spread-eagled on the floor.

The Monster. The Spectacle.

The Funeral Thief.

As I rose, people slowly retook their seats, all except for Connor, who glanced at me and winked. He clapped slowly and quietly, mouthing, "Well done, my good and faithful servant."

I was too exhausted to care.

Dad wrapped his arm around my warped back and hoisted me up, led me down the aisle, parting a sea of faces I partially recognized. He herded Ma and me into the last open row. "You okay?" he whispered.

"Yeah, but I can't stay here now." I panted. "I've messed up enough, haven't I?"

Dad exhaled hard. "I need to sit up front with the rest of the Circle. We'll leave right after the service."

I rubbed my face. "Yeah. Whatever." *Ashamed to sit by your freakish son, huh?*

Likely concerned that this change in plan might alter the created order, somehow circumventing the ham sandwiches that normally followed proceedings, Pastor Hildegard beelined for the pulpit. He opened his notes and his mouth, and at that instant the congregation came alive with mumbling. I'd heard that this type of ruckus occurred in Waxton Pentecostal, but never here, and good pastor Hildegard peered up and, after adjusting his glasses, squinted at the entrance behind me, the epicenter of the disturbance.

I forced myself around, and watched three men walk into the room. I'd never seen them before, which in this interconnected town meant nobody else in the room had either. They were old and jittery and dressed in identical black suits and hats. Creepy. Dad rose and, for the second time in minutes, walked down the aisle. He whispered to the first visitor, who took hold of Dad's elbow.

"Came to pay our respects." His reply was gentle. "News reached of the accident." The old guy sighed, like he really cared. "Shouldn't end this way for anyone."

By now, Mr. Cartwright had joined them in the aisle. He set a hand on Dad's shoulder, face aglow that even strangers would honor his daughter.

"You got that pegged right. You're more'n welcome to stay." He glanced down at me, and his eyes narrowed. "Move over, boy. Have you not been taught to make room for gentlemen?"

Truthfully, I had not. My appearances in church were few, usually following some inconsiderate behavior by Dad on Saturday night. Like the time he forgot to pick Ma up from Tulsa, after choosing to worship at the shrine of Sooner football. Did we not rise early the next morning to atone for his sin?

Ma and I slid to the wall, and soon the three creepies sat next to me. It wasn't long before they had all discovered the wayward wanderings of my spine.

If you've an infirmity or deformity and have endured harsh and obvious gawks, you know that pride somehow survives.

"What?" I hissed. "Never seen a back like this before?"

"No, Jonah, I guess I haven't," whispered my neighbor dressed in black. He paused, leaned over. "Where's Stormi?"

Oh, the power of a name, my name. It caused a deep, unsettled quaking. I blinked hard. "How do you know me?"

The pastor interrupted and launched into the remembrance talk. Filled with left-us-too-soons and we-don't-really-understands, the sermon was respectable, if not predictable. At least what I heard of it. My thoughts were fixed on the man seated to my left. He was dressed like an undertaker, and I didn't appreciate him knowing me so early in life.

The aroma of ham and potato salad wafted into the room, and the pastor brought the service to a speedy close. He hurried out the side door while those gathered mopped up with a very depressing rendition of "We Shall Overcome."

The last note sounded, and I turned to the stranger. "Okay, so now you can tell me how you know Stormi."

He glanced down at his hands. "She hasn't told you?"

"Told me what?"

"Good-bye, Mr. Everett."

He stood, fitted his hat, and slipped into the exiting flow.

"Hang on," I called.

The men did not turn, and by the time I hauled my body into the large meeting room, all three visitors had stepped out the front door.

I stood surrounded by crowds and conversation, conversations again sprinkled with my name. Twice, members of the hospitality committee offered me plates of food. Twice, I turned them down. Old Rickety had dampened my appetite. The strangers stole what remained.

"Jonah, what a dramatic opening to a funeral. Unusual." Arthur pushed toward me, caught me, shook my shoulders, and then quickly let go.

"You liked that?" I offered a quick smile, and lowered my voice. "Just trying to liven things up a little before I leave town tonight."

"Tonight? You do remember your promise—"

"Yes, Arthur. Your precious move." I pointed at the door. "Did you see those old guys?"

"Yes."

"Have you ever seen them before?"

"No."

"Right. And did you find them . . . unnatural or unusual or—"

"Unexpected."

"Yeah!" I grabbed his arm and he quickly pulled free. "Sorry, but they *were* unexpected, weren't they?"

He sighed as if my questions were boring him. "Yes. And they left because they didn't belong and they didn't know anybody."

I folded my arms. *Nobody except Stormi and me.*

"Jonah, come now!" Ma called from near the door and quickened her good-byes. She tugged on Dad, who looked tired of fielding seizure questions. They beckoned intensely and I grabbed a pillow mint and almost reached the door.

"Boy!" Mr. Cartwright and his wife weaved through a sociable crowd. Potato salad and ham sandwiches do wonders for the downtrodden. He planted himself squarely in front of me. "Where is she, son?"

First Creepy, now Cartwright.

"We had this talk already." Dad stepped forward. "You're not the only one eager to reach the bottom of this. When Jonah and Stormi return, we *all* have questions."

"We *all* didn't bury daughters," Mrs. Cartwright snapped.

"No," Ma said, her jaw tight. "Today, we didn't, but I can grasp the grief. There's nothing Jonah can do to ease it. He's had enough of his own pain today. You saw it yourself."

Mr. Cartwright grabbed my wrist and I grabbed Dad's, who grabbed Cartwright's. We stood there for a moment, firm gazes all around. Slowly, the pressure eased and I extracted my arm.

"You know what? Here's the ridiculous thing: Stormi didn't do anything to harm your daughter. She didn't," I said. "She tried to *save* Gina. But you can't wait to blame her for something. And you're in the Circle, so she's officially screwed." Ma tried to touch me, but I stepped back, my face hot. "Stormi tried to get everybody off that bus, including Gina, but Gina wouldn't move. In fact, she smacked Stormi with her textbook. There's the truth. Wasn't in the paper, but there it is. Your girl isn't here because she didn't move. That's all I know."

"Come, Jonah." Ma rounded my shoulder and whisked me out of the church, with Dad protecting our backside. "What's gotten into you?"

"Who else is going to stand up for her?" I spit out my mint. "Not Ms. P, not Cartwright, not Dad—"

Dad squeezed my shoulder, spun me, and stuck his finger into my chest. "Enough, Jonah."

"Well, are you?" I lowered his hand. "Sixteen kids told the Circle *exactly* the same story. And you're still going to put Stormi through an inquisition. How many witnesses do you need? Why are you so afraid of Cartwright?"

Dad's jaw tightened, and then loosened, releasing an exhale long and loud. "There are things in motion that you don't understand."

"*Bingovis! Absolutus!* So tell me, 'cause it seems really clear to me: you have seventeen breathing kids who owe their lives to Stormi."

Dad glanced at Ma. "Gina would have made eighteen."

Silence fell heavy, and I plodded home, knowing there would be no more words.

CHAPTER 8

"Your father and I have been thinking." Ma set the cling-wrap on the counter. She'd been following me around the kitchen. "Four seizures in one week. It's best you not head out alone."

I grabbed a root beer from the fridge. "Uh-huh."

"I'm also not tickled that you're heading out at night. Why not wait till the sun rises?"

"Uh-huh."

"Jonah! A little attention. You don't need to understand us, or even like us right now, but pay heed to sense. Let your father drive you to wherever you two are meeting."

"Oh, no." I stiffened. "You know every inch of my life, except this place. Wait, so tonight, you're hovering because of my seizures? You're worried about my safety?"

Ma leaned against the doorframe. "I'm hovering because you're in *my* kitchen, and I needed to prepare a tide-me-over for Tres." She paused. "And yes, contrary to what teens think, kids' seizures do steal a mother's sleep." Ma twisted her face around. "Is there another cause for concern?"

No. No, there wasn't, and the fact made me ill. Ma, self-appointed moral compass for the entire town of Gullary, and the unyielding, righteous buckle of the Bible belt, had no problem sending her eighteen-year-old son on an overnight with a beautiful eighteen-year-old girl.

How many times had she passed judgment on Connor for his nightly exploits? How many criticisms of Ms. P slipped from her lips, such as "That woman need keep a tight rein on that boy," and, "We all know what pulls at the bit of a young man"?

I blinked hard, and Ma rubbed her hands on her apron. "You all right?"

"Sure."

I was not, and as I stared at Ma, rage took root. She *shouldn't* feel at peace about Stormi. Wasn't I also a young man? Sure, I was deformed, and I'd been recently compared to Stormi's mother. Sure, I flopped and gagged, but I was still a guy—a good-looking one at that, aside from my torqued torso—and guys get ideas.

I'm a dangerous young man with dangerous urges.

I sighed. Or maybe not. Certainly my parents did not think it true. To them, I was barely male. I was a pitiful, lurching, castrated child, and Stormi another cute babysitter. No, Ma didn't say the words, but they rang clear in my mind: *My poor Jonah Everett. Take good care of my monstrous eunuch.*

I spun around, grabbed Tres's covered plate off the table, and walked by her outstretched arms. "Hug some other kid. I'll be back for my things. Don't wait up." I slammed the front door behind me and slumped back against it.

"Who am I kidding?" I thumped my head against the knocker and winced. "What right does a monster have to Stormi's affection?"

"I've never given thought to rights of monsters."

I jumped, temporarily losing hold on the tray, allowing corn to mingle with burrito meat. I calmed and rubbed my face hard when I saw it was Arthur. "You can't do that. You can't stand outside my home. That's called lurking"

His face was unaffected. "This is called assuring that my move will be made. I'm coming with you."

Arthur looked so determined, so settled on his course. He shifted his feet, as if bracing for a fight. Having been stripped of my manhood, no fight remained, and all I could do was sigh.

"Okay, but you need to stay in the gallery while I deliver the food and your instructions. That's a rule. Nobody follows me back there."

Arthur scrunched his face and adjusted the bridge of his glasses, fighting to loosen hold on his resolve. "That sounds reasonable."

We reached SMX, imposing by day and downright ominous beneath a pale moon. The yard lights stretched and warped my hunched shadow, enough so that Arthur stopped and pointed.

"You're basically a walking boomerang. A boomerang carrying a plate."

"Thank you, Arthur." I tongued my cheek. "You wanted me to move your pawn, right?"

"No. No! You can't mess this up!"

"That's what I thought." I smirked and removed the shark tooth necklace bearing the museum key from around my neck. I pushed into the gallery. "Here's where you wait." I switched on the lights and gestured around. "Feel free to browse. I won't be long. Odds are he's already asleep."

I opened the red door, and slid the brick in the crack.

"Jonah? That you, boy? Mighty late for a visit. Closin' in on midnight," Tres called. "You know how I be needin' my beauty sleep."

"You got that right." I shuffled to his cell. "Listen, I'm going off for a day or two. I don't know exactly who'll come to take my place—probably Dad—but Ma threw together a plate to hold you through in case provisions don't arrive in a timely manner. Burrito, I think."

"Mighty generous." He rose from his bed. "Where are you going, Jonah?"

"I can't say exactly, but I'm going to see Stormi."

"She left then. Without saying nothin'. No words. Nothin'."

I frowned, pushed my hand through my hair. "What was she supposed to say? She said enough in the note. Wait, that note. Yours and hers. They were the same."

"Huh." Tres began to pace. "Fancy that."

I set down the plate. "The same paper, Tres. Two halves, the same note. Can you explain that?"

"Not in a way that will bring you satisfaction." He glanced around the cell, cursing. "You done it now, Stormi."

"That's exactly what Stormi would say—well, the first part, not the cussing."

I watched and waited for Tres to explain his note trick, but minutes later he was still pacing.

"You know, it's late, so forget it, okay? Not a big deal. Probably a coincidence, that note." I stretched and released a mighty yawn. "The funeral took it out of me. Old Rickety showed up."

Tres slowed and took a deep breath. "I'm sorry 'bout that, Jonah. Really am."

"He wasn't the only visitor. Three old guys showed, never seen them before. They sat by me the entire time, and they knew me. At least my name."

"Hats?" Tres stopped pacing and looked off, gathering thoughts from somewhere else. When next he returned, his voice was a hair above a whisper. "Suits?"

"All."

Tres grabbed the bars and pressed his face through the opening, his eyes filled with urgency. "Do you trust me, son?"

I stepped nearer; don't know why, but I did. "I guess as much as any guy can trust a person he's known for six months, who's been locked up forever for doing some hideous thing, and who never shares a lick about his own life or what he's done or where he's been or . . . I mean, I trust you as much as that."

"That'll have to do." He reached out through the bars and his hand settled on my shoulder. Strong and gentle at the same time. "Time to lead. It's time for *you* to take the lead. She doesn't have courage without you."

Warmth spread down my arm. A good warmth. Wait, a seizure warmth? I quickly dropped to the floor just in case. "Crap. I gotta up my Tegretol. Two in a day? It's not helping a bit." The room spun and I closed my eyes. Shrieks and laughter invaded my dark, pressing so close, I felt the weight, the weight of a horror I didn't recognize.

And one voice that I did.

Tres.

"See you soon, Jonah."

I came to, aware I was on top of a bed. How I had traveled home was a mystery. I rolled over and wiped foam from my mouth and opened my eyes.

No.

Arthur sat staring at a chessboard, the chessboard inside Tres's cell, the cell that now held us and only us.

"Why are we here and where is Tres and all that?" I cleared my throat and tried again. "Are we locked in?"

"It would appear so." Arthur spoke, but did not turn. He was lost in the world of the game. Our incarceration was secondary.

I raised myself to an elbow, and then swung my feet over the edge.

"This can't have happened. What happened? Arthur! Look at me."

He rose from his kneel and rolled his eyes, as if releasing a prisoner was an acceptable outcome for the evening. He reached me a peanut-butter cookie, but I slapped it out of his hand.

"There's no need for that." He breathed deeply. "I had no choice. He told me I had no choice. He placed me in zugzwang."

"Don't start in with all that chess—"

"But I need to, because it explains our present situation." Arthur sighed and started to rock. "I did wait in the gallery, but you didn't come out, and didn't come out, and so finally I came in, and you were balled up on the floor."

"I know that part. I was occupied. But go on."

"I ran to help, and I met Tres. He wasn't at all like you described him. We talked for a while—"

"While I lay there jerking by your feet?"

"It's not a picture I would have chosen, but what was I supposed to do? Tres showed me the chessboard on the dresser, and told me it was nailed down. So I told him the move, and he said I must have forgotten the scheme. He said that I could not legally make that move. Jonah, I never forget the field of battle."

"No, I imagine you don't."

"But the pieces were too far away to prove it. He told me to come in and take a look. He told me there was a room where I could unlock all the cells."

"And you gave no thought to the fact that a prisoner was inviting you behind bars? Your powerful brain didn't think, 'Wow, what kind of idiot does he think I am?' or 'Maybe I should wait and ask Jonah?'"

Arthur glanced down and folded his hands. A puppy returned to the pound. My shoulders slumped. "Okay, I didn't . . . I really didn't mean the idiot thing."

"Yes, you did," he said quietly. "And I'm not. But Jonah, he said I was illegal, and I wasn't illegal. I would never be illegal." Arthur wiped a tear, and continued. "I opened the cell and showed him that it was fair, but he didn't care and quickly countered and then, well, he lifted you. All by himself, that old man lifted you gently onto that bed. Then he shut the door and left." Arthur pointed to the game board, now lowered onto a stand. "It wasn't nailed down."

"No."

"Maybe I am an idiot. Everyone says so. Even you."

"Not true." I tried the bars, and gave them a kick. "You are the most intelligent person I know. But we may be here for a time. Don't imagine Dad will come by until late tomorrow, and Ma will think I left straight away."

"That's fine. It will give me time to analyze his hasty play. See, I took his bishop. But then he took mine. It's a fool's move. It's a desperate move. He was winning. So now, with an exposed queen, he's conceded. At least I think he's conceded. Nobody that brilliant sacrifices a queen without cause."

"Jonah?" Stormi's voice echoed down the hall.

My heart leaped, and I pounded the bars. "Stormi! In here!"

"Is Tres?"

"No, he's gone."

Stormi's footsteps neared, and she froze in front of the cell. She glanced from our pen to the foul one beside it.

"Where is the old guy?" she asked, her gaze flitting down the hall. "Tell me you moved him to another cage. Tell me he's still in here somewhere."

"He's, uh, still in here somewhere."

I stared into her eyes and bit my lip. She already knew. "I didn't see it happen, Stormi. Honest. Old Rickety came and Arthur, well, it doesn't matter how Tres got out. But it would be really nice if you could open this cell." I quieted, searching as young men do for words, though words will never do. "It's good to see you."

Stormi threw back her hair and boot-kicked the bars. Once and again. "I can't believe you let this happen. Always trusting. Don't you ever *use* that crazy brain of yours? Does it, like, think? Like complete thoughts? Ever?"

Did my shoulders sag a little more? Did my heart shrivel? Of course, she was right, and I slinked back down onto the bed while Arthur told Stormi how to unlock the unit.

Five minutes later, she returned. Though my heart was no longer set on release, I slumped out and leaned against the wall across from the cell. Arthur hadn't moved. He scratched his chin and muttered at his game.

"You should have come to the old farm right away."

"I started to, and was unexpectedly delayed . . . You know what, forget it. You're right."

Stormi's face tightened. I'd never seen her cross, at least not with me. "We need to leave now, before daylight. And we can't go to the farm anymore, it's too nearby, what with the old guy loose. Do you know some place far away where we could disappear?"

We. She said *we.* She was furious and I had been stupid, but she still wanted to be with me. I stood and straightened, well, as much as possible.

"Yeah, disappearing is probably best. Wait. What? Disappearing from Gullary? For how long?"

Stormi said nothing, but reached her hand toward me, eyes pleading.

I stared long at her gently beckoning fingers. My friend needed me, and for no other reason that should have been enough, but it wasn't. My hand balled, grasping familiar, anxious thoughts. Will I seize today? Tomorrow? My heartbeat quickened. Vanishing was all well and good for Stormi; what daily battles did she fight?

How little I knew.

I opened my hand too slowly, and Stormi's flopped to her side. "I need you, Jonah."

"Oh!" Arthur shot up and tossed me a balled-up sheet. "Tres told me to pass this on. He said it's his next few moves."

"I'm kind of in the middle of a moment. Besides, I doubt he's coming back." I tossed the paper back.

Arthur unfolded the paper and scowled. "Guys?"

"We need to leave." Stormi stomped toward the red door, pausing to cast me a hopeful glance before disappearing into the gallery.

I sighed and gestured to Arthur. "A little speed. I have to lock—"

"There's a problem." Arthur adjusted his glasses. "It says, 'Truth with three hats and suits. Avoid Q to prevent more loss. Suggested next moves: J3 and S1 to Bishop.'"

"So what's the prob—Wait, three hats and suits? What color are you playing?"

"Black."

Black.

"Okay, so make his move, and what would be your next logical play?"

"That's the thing. I can't follow his directions." He stepped out of the cell. "There are no chessboard squares labeled J3 or S1."

I rubbed my face and shook my head. "I, uh, have to let this craziness go. Stormi is waiting on me and—"

"But, I do have some friends with those names," Arthur said quietly. "J3: Jonah the third. S1: Stormi the, well, the first, I guess. Looks like Tres wants you to go to Bishop."

"Bishop, Oklahoma? That's hundreds of miles away. In the panhandle."

Stormi poked her head through the door. "Jonah!"

"Coming."

Arthur and I walked briskly down the hall. He paused to press the captured black bishop into my hand. "So what's your play?"

I glanced at the piece. "Are you ever afraid?"

Arthur frowned, and I waved him off.

"She said we need to disappear, someplace far away . . ." I tucked the bishop into my pocket. "I never would have thought of it myself, but now I think I know the place."

CHAPTER 9

Stormi was beautiful when angry.

Beautiful, but not quiet.

I was the recipient of a strange peace. Stormi's yellow pick-up sped west out of Gullary, and miles quickly separated me from the oddness of the funeral and Tres's escape. The anxiety that plagued me seemed somehow connected to the fabric of Gullary, and the more I ripped free, the less weight remained to smother me. Stormi's mind clearly found no similar rest, racing in bursts around the same chaotic track. Fits of rage gave way to nervous chatter, followed by lengthy pauses. Rage, fear, repeat.

I hoped for a moment that Stormi might return to herself, to someone I knew. I hoped and sat silent. What do you do when the rock in your life turns buoyant and starts bouncing in the waves? You hunch forward to relieve the pressure on your vertebrae, lean hard against the door, and wait.

At least that's what I did.

". . . Jonah! Are you even listening to me?"

"Okay, yeah." I straightened, sort of. "I've been lost in thought. Sorry. But definitely listening to you while I was lost in the thoughts." I rubbed my temple, urging away an oncoming headache. "Are you okay? I mean, I can't remember you ever losing it like that."

"You made me lose it!"

"I was writhing on the floor. You can't cut me a little slack?"

"You want sympathy."

"No, I just don't think I deserve *all* the blame." I folded my arms. "Maybe two percent, two percent of the blame."

Stormi opened her mouth to speak, then closed her lips.

"I'd go as high as six percent," I said.

"Six percent," she repeated and shifted, and for a moment her anger ebbed. "There are things I haven't told you, Jonah." She glanced down, and the truck swerved. When we regained the road, Stormi had all but lost her voice. "A lot I haven't said."

It was my turn to get upset, and I really tried. After all, I told Stormi everything . . . well, except for my postal felonies. She took my secrets and she held back. Thief! Liar! But none of those accusations worked. I felt no betrayal. I glanced at her face, and a new shade had taken over, one not seen in all my years of studying and yearning.

She seemed frail, broken . . . human. I wanted to touch her—not for the fantasy it promised me, but for the comfort it might give her. Somehow, her being human made me more human too.

"You could tell me a secret or two now, if you wanted. It's just us."

Nothing.

"Or you could ignore the *Deformicus beasticus* at your side—"

"Shut up."

"Or you could verbally abuse the deformed beast at your side."

Stormi slammed the brakes and swerved onto the shoulder. She turned and stuck her finger in my chest. "*You* aren't a beast." She poked harder, her nail discovering soft tissue. "*You* never were." She fisted up and smacked my shoulder, deadening my arm. "It's me. I'm the beast. Can't you see it?"

None of what she was saying made a lick of sense, but I kept my tongue planted.

She collapsed into my chest, and I awkwardly placed my arms around her. Such foreign territory. I had nothing to offer. There had been strange moments before when she'd requested closeness, but it never felt like *I* was required. I was simply the nearest armed creature.

But not here. No other set of headlamps was in sight, and with the wind shuddering the truck and an odd fear filling her words, I felt suddenly as though it was me she wanted. No one else. The idea was strangely warming.

"I can't see anything, Storm. You know that. You said that." I buried my face in her hair. "Besides, I'm six percent responsible for this mess. I'm the gullible one, remember, the crooked painting that'll never hang straight. But you, you're the beauty, at least that's how I figure it."

She tensed in my arms, but did not pull away. "Promise me that when you find out, you won't leave me."

"Find out what?"

"Promise me."

"Yeah, I promise."

She scooched away, and wiped her eyes with the heels of her hands. She reached forward and gently lifted my chin. "Jonah, you are gullible."

We eased back onto a different road, me and the stranger beside me, the one who looked like Stormi but who spoke in confused tones like mine. Confused words. Unhinged words.

Morning came, fled, and we sunk deeper into the dryness of afternoon. Although it was still spring, the horizon shimmered in the heat. With no AC in the truck, it was too hot to talk, and the distance between us lengthened. Another hour passed, and the heat flat-out baked away whatever affection Stormi's midnight embrace revealed.

"I'm going to pull off for gas," Stormi said.

"Yeah, I could use a stop."

Stormi looked at me with questioning eyes. Our relationship was changing, but I couldn't figure how.

The Wanaka exit fast approached. Wanaka consisted of one Shell station, Wanaka Liquors, and Jethro's Antique Emporium, and we sidled up to the lone gas pump. Another truck was mid-fill on the opposite side, and Stormi exhaled hard.

"You pump, I pay, or . . ."

"Naw, I need the facilities inside." I pushed out. "I'll cover it. Put in thirty."

"Be quick," she called with urgency.

An odd command, as one has limited control over a bladder's demands.

Odd commands. Stiff red flags I rarely ignored.

Rarely.

I strolled through the door, pausing to stretch my spine, before tracking down the bathroom. I slumped inside. It's a mindless affair, standing before a urinal after hours of languishing in a truck. Thoughts drift over the miles, and this trip provided little to latch on to. Stormi had come strangely unglued, which unnerved me, yet not as much as I would have thought.

Business done, I washed and power dried and wandered out toward the bubble-gum-chewing kid behind the counter. He couldn't have been older than me, and he certainly paid me no mind, lost as he was in his Superman comic book.

Two scruffy guys jostled around the freezer, and I suddenly felt sick, strange sick. Like I was in a scene from a movie sick. It wasn't the scruff—I was familiar with dirt and wear from a life in Gullary—no, it was the volume. No-goods who possessed the decency to hush their antics, well, there was rarely much harm in them. It was the others who, like Connor, felt no shame and broadcast their no-goodness. That's who you had to fear.

In that instant, I thought to check on Stormi, but I was hypnotized, my gaze captured by a couple of idiots laughing and shoving.

"What you staring at?" The older one turned and took a step toward me.

I broke free. "Nothing. Staring spell. Go on back to whatever." Eager to be out and done, I glanced at the counter and the door, and was once again captured.

Posted smack in the middle of the glass, right above the *Sorry, We're Closed* sign, was a poster the size of a newspaper, a Wanted poster.

Though hastily printed off by a machine badly in want of toner, the three faces were frighteningly recognizable.

The largest mug belonged to Tres. Tres Cantor. The warning stretched beneath his name.

Considered armed and dangerous. Do not attempt to apprehend. Call Authorities immediately.

Beneath Tres, side by side, Stormi and me.

"Stormi Pickering. Granddaughter of the above. Jonah Everett III. Friend of the above."

I backed away from the counter, and glanced over my shoulder at bubble-gum boy still lost in his comic. I quietly removed the poster and pushed outside. "Stormi! You've got to see—"

Stormi was pressed up against the pump, arms pinned above her head, a defiling knee wedged between her legs. The guy from the other truck moved against her, his head performing such acts with her neck that to think of them still makes me wince.

Thoughts flew through my head. The no-goods would soon be here, making escape impossible. Bubble-Gum couldn't see, didn't want to see, any of this. Rage filled me.

"Hey!" I lurched toward the scuffle, scanned my options, and grabbed the nozzle from Stormi's truck. I yanked the rear of the Defiler's jeans with all the authority I owned, and jammed the pump nozzle down deep into the back of his pants.

Words I will not record flew from his mouth. He spun, first to swing at me, and when I ducked, he fought and clawed at his backside.

"Go! Go!" I hollered, and Stormi raced around to the passenger's side of the truck, while I leaped his wildly swinging gassy tail and pitched myself into the driver's side. From the building, voices exploded as the other two raced out, shouting.

Ignition. Gas pedal. Our tires spun in the gravel as the Defiler finally extracted the hose. Treads caught and we fish-tailed forward. I checked the rearview. Bubble-Gum was jogging toward the three, all of whom pointed in our direction.

I drove. Kept driving. My breath fought out, while my heart beat wildly.

"I can't believe it! Stormi, I couldn't hear you. I didn't hear your scream, or I would have been there quicker, I should have . . . I got lost in there, and then there you were . . ."

"I didn't scream. Did you pay for the gas?" Stormi asked quietly.

"What? Gas? No. Who cares? Are you okay? That guy, I mean those guys would have, you know, he didn't look like stop was on his mind."

"He wouldn't have been the first."

117

I knew what she meant. And then I didn't. "Wait, he wasn't the first to try, you know, or he wasn't the first . . . period?"

"Look at me," she said softly. "What do you think?"

There was a right answer. I knew there was. I also knew this was a time for listening and being there and all that crap you learn in psychology. I should have been thinking only of her, of what she went through, but anger brought out the ugly and twisted all goodness. My eyes stung.

"So why do you climb in the car with every stupid guy who asks? There's me and Connor off that list, but that's pretty much it. Do you think they care, like, at all? Do you know how guys talk and what they say? Well, I don't, because I can't handle listening to them. What do they tell you? That they need you? Love you?

"If you don't believe me, listen to the guy who you think of like a mother. How can you see everything and be so dang blind?"

"Oh. My. God," she whispered.

We drove for two silent hours. There was no way to fix it, fix us. I drove and hoped for a seizure to come and end the misery.

"Do you enjoy my letters?"

Her voice so cold, so distant.

"No . . . yes. I read a bunch of them." *Stop. Stop. Leave it.* "I thought you'd be happy. At least they reached your mother." I shook my head. I couldn't stop digging.

"Good. I'm glad you enjoyed them. Since we're coming clean, you selfish ape, I go out to prove to myself that my *no* still works, to remind myself that I'm worth . . . I'm worth it. You should stick around and listen to the fools in the locker room. Listen to what they say about me. Listen to what they can't say."

"Who says you're not worth—"

She glanced sharply at me and swallowed hard and I knew.

Had Connor been here, I would have at least tried to kill him. But he wasn't. It was just me and my pain, and I didn't know how to kill that.

"Connor tries to take," Stormi said resolutely. "But if you speak his name again, I will find some way to kill you."

"You just did."

Stormi blinked hard. "It shouldn't be hard to forget him. We're not going back."

"Whatever." My mind whirred. "Wait. What about my parents? Ms. P? Of course we'll go back." I veered off the road, regained composure, and slowed. "Won't we?"

Stormi reached down between us, gently lifted the poster that had found its way into the truck, and flattened it over her thighs. She placed it so I could see it. "You didn't pay for gas. Now they have our license plate for sure, they know this truck, they'll know where I live. They'll look for us there, and when they do . . ." She pointed at the photo of Tres. "We'll have bigger problems."

"How is he bigger than what happened? And Con . . . the nameless guy? What is going on?" I rubbed my face with a gas-scented hand. "What bigger problems?"

She was gone again, and I swallowed hard. How many hurtful things can a guy say in one conversation?

"And Tres." I forced a smile. "What idiot thought he was your grandfather?"

In the distance, a lit-up squad car screamed nearer. It raced by, leaving a trail of sound.

"Stormi? I'm sorry, Stormi."

"Turn off when you can." She straightened. "It's time that we talk."

Clouds gathered quick and ominous, and we drove off the main road, deeper into the hills. We'd left the wombing cover of the Ozarks back in Gullary, and I knew what lay west: they didn't call it No Man's Land without cause. Red dirt, tumbleweed, stretches of flat, and winds that stole your sight. A chest flutter sounded an anxious note. I was leaving all I knew, risking a future on the girl I suddenly didn't. Not going back?

This hadn't been part of my plan, well, Tres's plan.

We wound through the gentle hills. My mind felt solid, but my dumb heart was broken.

Connor. I knew it.

Stormi scanned this way and that, asking me to slow at each rundown farmstead. I wasn't sure what she was looking for, but one peek at that sky and I knew we didn't have time to be choosy.

The storm gust hit, pushing the truck off line and onto the chatter strips lining the shoulder. Stormi jumped.

"Keep on the road, Jonah."

"We need to get off the road. There's swirling up there. We need shelter."

Stormi closed her eyes. "Turn in to the next place. It'll be vacant."

I took a quick right and snaked onto a property so decrepit, fears of breaking and entering vanished. We scrambled out and blew toward the boarded-up front porch.

"Busted window!" I pointed.

"Go inside." Stormi pushed me forward. I wedged my spine through the opening and tumbled in, landing with a thud on hardwood. Stormi did not follow.

"Stormi?" I winced and stared out the window. She walked into the distance, lit like a strobe in the afterglow of lightning strikes. Rain poured down on arms spread-eagled. Her face was upturned, soaking in the wet.

"You'll get killed out there," I called, but my voice was feeble.

She needs you.

I heard it, plain as plain, but my legs were rooted. The next bolt cracked nearby, and by this time Stormi had fallen to the ground. She pounded the earth again and again, screaming into the night. I'd spent hours staring at her curtain, but this felt so private, so agonizing, I couldn't watch, and slumped down to the floor.

Stormi fell apart, and I was afraid.

She needs you.

When next I peeked, she stood at the window, soaked and shivering, tears streaming down her face. I backed up as she crawled in and fell into my arms. We found the corner and huddled, as ancient boards creaked with each gust.

Forever passed, and in the blackness of the main room, I stared up.

"Do you think she'll hold?"

Stormi's breath came in staccato bursts. "Yes." Her hand found my arm in the dark.

There are places filled with memory, where the past hangs thick like dough. This old place was like that, refusing to crumble, though countless storms had certainly come to call. Ma would say the spirit was strong in those walls. Stormi seemed to be fighting that spirit. Finally, the words.

"Let me talk, and don't interrupt. Let me get this out while I can, here, where you can't see me."

"Yeah, sure."

She smacked my arm, but in the darkness her fist glanced off my shoulder and cuffed me across the jaw. "I said, don't interrupt." Again, Stormi gripped my forearm.

"But—"

She released me long enough to smack again, and I held my tongue. Soon she softened, laying her head on my lap.

"Have you ever felt summoned?"

"Dad was summoned for jury once, down to Tulsa."

"Shut up!"

"Sorry, it just sounded like a question."

The storm crackled overhead, and above us, the busted chandelier tinkled. Each remaining shard of dew-drop glass reflected the sky's light show, creating a disco ball effect. The flashes were tough on an epileptic, but my mind remained my own, and I waited, and waited.

"I got the first letter when I was ten. Remember Danny?"

Of course I did. Dad fired him from the gallery without cause—well, without good cause. Truth is, Dad needed a job for me. Danny was gone from Gullary the next day, and nobody had heard from him since.

Stormi continued, "He hand delivered it."

"I'm not following." I slapped my hand over my mouth.

She sighed. "Tres wrote to me. When I was a little girl, he introduced himself. Of course I showed it to Martha, and she had the test done immediately."

"Test?"

"A grandparentage test. It turned out Tres was my grandpa after all."

I winced my back into a new position. "You're kidding! Well, that's great, right? I mean, you actually know someone from your family! You know, maybe a violent-convict-type of family member, but still . . ." She was silent. "That is great, isn't it?"

More lightning.

"His letters started coming every week." Stormi tapped my thigh, slow and metered. "Each one ended the same. 'Do your job, Stormi. And whatever you do, don't get hooked up with that Jonah.'"

"Me?"

"No. The other Jonah. Of course you." She exhaled, and her voice softened. "But I did. I fell for Jonah."

"Me?"

Another smack. "Don't go there. Not now. Tres wrote more than once that you'd keep me from 'carrying through my summons.' He said that the more I felt for you, the less I'd see. The less I'd let myself see." Stormi paused. "But I was ten. None of it made sense. It does now. Tres was right. I feel it. I was summoned, and I think Tres was the one who called me, called me to do something, something big and important and terrible, but I can't see it, Jonah. I still can't. And you're all rolled up in it. But all I see is you."

"Me?"

"Could you use another word?"

"Uh—"

"Then you took over at the museum. Tres took to you. He was pulling you in, and it scared me, but I figured, what could he do to you from behind bars? But now . . ."

I tried to reason out her story, but I kept getting stuck at the same point.

"You felt for me?" I asked.

Stormi sat up. "Seriously? That's all you heard of what I said?"

"Well, not all, but it seems to be the sticky part—good sticky, you know? Well, sticky isn't really the right word. Maybe consequential is a better word. Consequential with hopeful implications. Right? Or not."

She started to stand and I grabbed her arm. "Hang on, I'm pressing out the me part and now do recall the rest. Let me get this straight. We're running from Gullary, because tooth-less Tres, from inside his cell, called you forth from wherever you came from and placed you down in a sleepy town to do something terrible, but you couldn't do it because of me. Now you're scared that, what, he'll find us and gum us to death?" I chuckled. She didn't, and I cleared my throat. "You said it yourself—he's just an old guy."

"He's more than that."

I shivered. Because I knew she was right. Like Stormi, he also knew too much. He may have slept behind bars, but I couldn't recollect a conversation in which he wasn't in control.

The door rattled hard, and Stormi scampered to her feet. "He's here," she whispered.

"The wind is here," I whispered back.

She pulled me into the kitchen, and then beneath the table. "No, he's found us. He's been following us the entire time."

From outside, "Jonah." My name swept away with the wind, but I had heard it.

"Tres." I sustained the whisper. "Your grandpa is not going to kill us. He had a chance and he didn't."

I climbed out from beneath the table, walked toward the window, and froze. A silhouette, dark against dark, stood in the room.

"I tried the door, but you didn't answer, so then I tried the window. This might be illegal. I've never been illegal before."

"Arthur? What are you . . . ? How did you . . . ?"

He shifted, and in the dark I could tell he walked on unfamiliar footing. "You're a friend. I have to warn you. You and Stormi are in a fierce zugzwang."

CHAPTER 10

"Something murky is happening in Gullary."

Arthur sat at the kitchen table, staring out the broken window. The wind and rain relented, and we joined him in the darkened room.

"The older ones are scared. My parents. Your parents. And those older still. Everyone is scared, and everyone is talking about you and the prisoner. A bunch have set out after you. Some want to bring you back, and then there's Mr. Cartwright." Arthur pulled a candy bar from his pocket, removed the wrapper, and took a large bite. "He's why I'm here."

"Cartwright?" Stormi tensed; I could feel it even in the dark.

Another big chocolate bite. Arthur nodded. "He was going door to door asking everyone if they knew where you were. I couldn't have him ask me. I would have had to tell him what I suspected."

"Why?" Stormi asked.

"He just would," I answered.

"So I had to leave, because I knew."

"And you found us in an abandoned house?"

His chewing slowed. "I don't have a good explanation. I drove past a gas station, saw commotion, and knew I was close. I knew you'd get off the highway. But I kept driving until the storm and, I don't know, I felt summoned. Then there was Stormi's truck."

"Summoned? By who?" I turned to Stormi, who slowly shook her head.

"So Arthur used a familiar word, a really unusual, coincidental word. It doesn't mean anything. It doesn't mean Tres had anything to do with him finding us. And, Stormi, none of what you said means we should be afraid of the guy, but Gullary is. Do you know anything else? What did he do? What does he know?"

Ringing in my ears drowned out her answer, and I slumped to the floor. Old Rickety was also summoned, and had his sights aimed directly at me. He struck with a force I hadn't experienced in years. There was no gradual lead in—no easing into hell—and my brain raised the white flag without a fight.

I was out.

I came to in the truck, with my head bouncing against the passenger side window. Stormi drove with purpose, and Arthur sat squeezed in between. Control of my mouth didn't return to me for some time, but thoughts that made little sense flooded in.

Arthur found us.

Tres was looking for us.

Stormi hated Tres.

Stormi liked me.

Stormi liked me? A drip of spittle fell from my mouth, traced down my chin. All her teasing was real? No, locker room stories about her; they were real. How could she fall for the monster? She deserved someone better. Or maybe I did.

I am never going home.

The thought rattled around in my mind. A life on the run. A life with Stormi. Never going home. The idea didn't shock me. It didn't frighten me, and the wildness of it would have made me smile were I in control of my mouth. Bonnie and Clyde. Stormi and Jonah.

With faithful sidekick Arthur.

We bumped on through the night.

"There." Arthur pointed at the turnoff. "There's the sign. Bishop, Oklahoma. That's where we need to go."

Stormi lowered her voice. "Why Bishop? Jonah still hasn't told me. He only said he knew a place."

I peeked at Arthur. I could see him thinking, trying to find a truth that wouldn't get me killed.

"It just played out that way."

Stormi was quiet. "Okay, then."

Well done, Arthur. Well done.

Bishop, Oklahoma
The Jewel of Red Carpet Country
Population 102

Stormi rumbled to a stop at the hand-painted sign on decaying wood, ominous in the headlamp's beam. "Are you back, Jonah?"

I blinked my eyes. Sleep must've found me, and I pushed myself higher, peered around.

"Yeah, that was a tough one. Sorry. Can you see the town?"

Stormi slowly shook her head. She knew what I knew; we'd reached the end of the world, the Oklahoma panhandle.

Though I'd never been, we spent a good deal of time discussing the panhandle in school. That Bishop was nowhere to be seen on any map did not surprise me; panhandle history was filled with places that were, and then weren't.

Okie towns disappeared for many reasons. Those in the northeast vanished due to the poison man dug up. But panhandle ghost towns, they just blew away. Some started as Native American settlements. Tribes held the land gently, loosely, letting the ground shift like the sand dunes near Beaver. White folk thundered in, determined to fix those towns to earth. The lack of trees should've been the tell; panhandle roots don't stretch down deep.

When times got hard, when the dust came, people blew away, leaving remnants, remnants of lives. Soon the wind reclaimed the remnants, leaving no trace of man.

Except perhaps this population sign.

Arthur spotted it first, a dot of light in the distance. After a nod from me, Stormi eased toward a bar that seemed to rise out of the earth. We pulled up, our truck awash in dust, and joined near thirty others parked every which way, headlamps on full. That was it. This was the dramatic culmination of Tres's plan.

Bishop consisted of one bar.

Moonlight refracted in the glimmer of those headlamps, casting mini rainbows all around. When the wind died, it shone down large and bright, and to each horizon, the world turned flat. No hills to cover us or valleys to shield us. No trees. Just space, wide and dark and lonely. And a lit-up bar.

"What exactly made you think this would be a good place to hide?" Stormi chewed a nail.

I couldn't tell her that we were here because of Tres, because he had suggested it.

"I knew Bishop was in the panhandle, that it was far away without being too far." I waited, knowing Stormi would sense the stupid in my answer. But she didn't. She scanned the jostling kids—most of them seemed a whisker above drinking age—bit her lip, and shrugged.

"Tell me where to go," Stormi said quietly.

"I think inside."

And with the direction came the thought. I had no idea why we were here. Not one to follow without cause, I had done so given Tres's directions. In that way, he was a bit like Stormi—authoritative—and I hadn't questioned.

Until now.

We pulled into the parking lot, which looked little different than the plain around it, and quieted the engine. Stormi and Arthur both turned to me, and I forced a smile. "This can't be all of Bishop, right?"

I pushed out of the truck and stretched. Long drives took a toll on my spine and I forced it vertical. I weaved through the laughter. It wasn't directed at me, I knew that, but it cut just the same. A lonely hurt. An outside-looking-in hurt. It had been that way in Gullary, when kids would gather and I would stumble on their mockery.

Here, the three of us passed through like ghosts. Unseen. Unnoticed.

"Hey, girl!"

Well, two of us passed on through.

Stormi's hand found mine, and she pulled me onto the porch and inside.

We stood blinking in the doorway. It was silent, motionless, as if the place had somehow been turned inside-out. There was a bar on the right, a bartender reading a paper behind it, and three haggard men sprinkled about the tables.

I shrugged and wandered up to the barkeep, still gripping Stormi's hand. "Excuse me. Is this Bishop?"

"Pretty much." The guy didn't look up. He shifted his readers, stroked his gray stubble, and yawned. "Can leave 'm on the pile."

A stack of church bulletins, stained and dog-eared, rested to his left.

"I don't have one."

"Hmm. Your loss. What didn't happen in church this morning, we'd have got done for you tonight. Free drink in exchange for your church bulletin. Maybe go find one and come on back."

I'd never seen a man so wholly disinterested, so vacant, but I had questions that needed answering.

"If we wanted to find a place to stay nearby, where'd we look?"

"That be dependin' on your definition of nearby." He removed his glasses and set down his paper. Checking us over, his gaze landed on Stormi and stayed there. He glanced over my shoulder at the men seated in the bar and lowered his voice. "You seem a piece more desperate than most drivin' to Cimarron. Plenty o' places you shouldn't stay in these here parts. Move on. Quick and quiet. There's a Super 8 in Boise City not sixty miles west, near the mesa."

"We could make that," I said, turning to Stormi. Post-seizure exhaustion was sinking in, and my judgment was turning foul. Sure, I had originally chosen Bishop, but Stormi counted on me to provide safe quarters, especially after the events at the station.

"Seems quite a trip this late. You look tired."

We spun around in time to see a clean-shaven man in his thirties rise from his table. I hadn't noticed him before.

"I know a place not eight miles from here. It's no Super 8, but it provides two beds. And believe you me, it's private."

I glanced at Stormi and back, mustering my strength. "We need three beds. We're not really together."

He let his gaze run over Stormi. "There's a shame."

"I mean in the sense of together that you might think we're, or two of us are, together—"

"Two beds would be wonderful." Stormi wrapped her arm around my twisted trunk.

A whisper in my ear. "You don't want to be going where he'd be taking you. Death there." But when I turned, the bartender was back behind his paper.

"What's the name of the place?" I asked.

The man walked up to us and reached out his hand, first to Arthur, then to Stormi, and finally to me. "Names are nothing compared to what it offers. Seclusion. A place for the weary to find rest." He gestured toward the front door. "Out away from the world and all that comes with it. It's up to you, of course, but there'd be minimal cost and you could up and on your way whenever you so choose." He paused. "Nothing asked. Nothing required."

I froze. I'd heard that phrase before.

"So it's not a hotel? How do we know it's safe?" Arthur whispered far too loudly.

"Safe? Is that what you're looking for? I s'pose you can't know for sure. But young folk don't come out here to be found, they come out here to get lost, and that, friends, I can guarantee."

The three of us huddled, but nobody spoke. It was a horror movie set-up. But our truck would soon be located, which meant a hasty shipment back to Gullary, and Stormi would have nothing of it.

"What's your name?" Stormi asked.

"Sixty-one."

"Your name's a number?" I asked.

"Your given name," Stormi asked, her voice firm and terrible.

His face twitched, as if fighting a return to some place he should not go. "Winston."

She stepped toward him, holding him in that horrible Stormi gaze. "Nothing asked."

He smiled. "Nothing required."

Stormi turned to me. "We need to go where Tres will lose our trail. This is our chance."

"I thought you didn't believe in chance."

Stormi peeked at Winston. "We'll follow you."

Arthur and Stormi wandered toward the door, and behind me a paper rustled furiously. I glanced over my shoulder, and the bartender caught my eye. "Be gone by morning. You don't want to meet Q."

I frowned and followed my friends out into the night, my fingers grasping the chess piece in my pocket.

Q. The queen?

Avoid Q to prevent more loss. Tres's note read itself in my mind.

This was my second warning. Yeah, by morning we would be gone. One way or another.

Our destination snuck up on us like a star-eating mass, a dark collection of lightless structures that blocked out horizon-hugging constellations. We followed Winston's truck to a row of garages, and he hopped out and lifted a door. He waved us in, and Stormi obliged, parking behind a white Chevy. Winston quickly pulled in behind us.

The garage was built three cars deep, and we were wedged in the middle.

We would not be gone in the morning.

"I don't like anyone who gives his name as a number. Is that even legal?" Arthur shook. He was losing it. "I don't like staying with strangers. I don't like anything about—"

"Arthur!" Stormi said. "It'll be okay. Jonah brought us here. It'll be okay."

"Now hold on, there's a little error in that narrative. You okay'd the sleeping situation. You said, and I quote, 'We'll follow you.' It's not like I had much to do with us coming *here*, as in, right here. Bishop, yep, but I was tilting Super 8. But you, when you get all confident and Stormi-voiced, it usually means, you know, you have it under control."

Stormi stroked her necklace. "I don't have anything under control, Jonah. I can't feel anything. We're following you."

"I'm following you, Jonah. I'm right behind you."

I had been on my way home from Percival's, Gullary's food mart/video store/dry cleaner. Folded over my left forearm was a suit, on the eve of my first suit-wearing occasion, the spring formal.

The dance had once been a prom—at least in the old yearbooks, it was called a prom—but something foul must have happened in 1980, because in 1981, there was no yearbook, and in '82, the event had become a highly militarized spring formal. It remained so right up to my senior year.

I wanted to survive it, survive my first and only trip to it.

Of course I was going with Stormi. She would look beautiful. I'd forced in the thought of her, and pressed out the voice of Connor, striding three feet behind me. Why he was trailing me home, I could not say, other than the cruelty of man.

"They have strobe lights. Strobe lights cause them seizures, right? That would be embarrassing."

Think about Stormi.

"It'd be a sight, seeing you foam all over her."

I stopped and turned. "Why? Why do you do this to me?"

Connor licked his lips, reached out, and snatched my suit. He gently laid it on the ground, and dug his muddy heels into it. Again and again. Then he carefully picked it up, folded it over my arm, and walked away. "Have a nice evening, Hunch."

Why had I watched? Why didn't I make a move to protect what was mine?

Why had I been so weak?

I showed up at the dance two hours later, my black suit blotched with oil, my red tie and once-white shirt the same. Yeah, I wore the outfit. I felt I deserved it. That somehow the grotesque covering matched the gruesome interior.

Chaperones manned the three escapes from Gullary Golf's nine-hole public clubhouse. Chaperones wandered among the dancers, enforcing the bodily contact rule with vigor. But it still appeared to be the highlight of most students' year.

Stormi stood by herself beneath the disco ball. I think the other girls kept distance, as compared to her, all their fashion efforts paled. She stood waiting for me in a short, deep red dress, which swished gently over her beautiful thighs and was hemmed beneath her knees. I figured right there that the red dress would pretty much destroy every other couple's chance at enjoying the event; for a guy, to see Stormi that night was to want her.

I know I did.

It mattered little. Old Rickety took me by the punch bowl before the first dance. Soon I was drenched, tinted orange, and carted home by my dad.

Apparently, Stormi stayed and danced the night away.

I'm glad she got to enjoy the senior formal. It was a really pretty dress.

I came to in blackness.

Stormi had hold of my left hand, the one I could feel. The right was still numb, along with that side of my body.

"Welcome back." Stormi smiled. "Sorry we didn't get that dance." Her voice softened. "I'm also sorry I didn't stay with you. It still could have been a great night."

I glanced at her, my mouth unable to speak. She must have been recounting the night of the formal. Somehow her words pressed in, even while I writhed in the garage.

"How would . . ." I fought through the fog. "How would it have ended?"

Stormi leaned over and kissed my ear. "With you and me."

"It always ends with you and me, but it never starts that way."

Her head paused, her hair falling over my face. "Don't start this now."

"I never do."

Stormi straightened and gave my hand a squeeze. "No, you don't. You could have a thousand times, but you don't. You're the only gentleman I know."

"It hurts to be me."

"I know, Jonah."

We fell silent in the dark, and I thought I might have caught her sniffing, but my senses still weren't trustworthy, and I lay still beneath her touch.

"Well, Winston wasn't lying. Two beds," Stormi whispered, and nearby Arthur snored. She looked off. "The other is already claimed."

I was so tired, the implication didn't strike me until morning, when I woke with Stormi nestled in the crook of my arm.

How could she see me at my most disgusting and still come near? How could she embrace a monster? That kind of affection only lived in moms and God, and I wasn't even sure about that.

But she was here, and I leaned over and smelled her hair.

"Do you enjoy irony?"

Arthur stood in the corner, posture impeccable, his hands folded in front of him. Maybe he was off somehow. When it came to Arthur, maybe God had withheld or given too much or just plain got tired of cookie-cutter personalities. But his back; it was beautiful. He was beautiful. Straight and solid. Vertebrae lined up like soldiers at attention, ready for any order.

Sure, I held the girl, but in that instance, would I have traded my support for his?

I'm ashamed of my answer.

"Irony," he continued, far too loudly. "You came to this place to flee Tres, who you think brought you here."

I frowned. Put like that, it was clear: Tres had hopped off the edge of my life and run to the center. He was the reason for everything. I slowly pointed toward Stormi and mouthed, "She doesn't know that."

"Irony number two. For the second time in as many days, you and I are trapped in a cell together."

"I wouldn't call this a cell. It's comfortable enough."

"It's a cell. What kind of people get a place to stay for free and aren't asked to do anything?"

"Uh . . ."

"Prisoners, which makes this a cell. It has a pretty girl inside, but it is still a cell."

"I think you're jumping to conclusions."

"And, since nobody walks into their own cells—"

I thought of Mom. Presumably, she chose to walk down the aisle with Dad.

"You're wrong."

"No, I'm not. Nobody walks into their own cell. They are always led."

"You're still wrong."

"So," he continued, "we've not been choosing. We must've been led, and people who lead need to know a little more than those who follow. We've been led by someone . . ." He lowered his voice; not low enough, "Who knows events before we do."

I squinted and pointed at Stormi. "What? Storm—? No. She's terrified. She's running. She's following me. Said so herself."

"She followed *you* here?"

"Well, it's not quite how I remember it, but she said she did."

Arthur grinned a very knowing grin. "I think you may be in bed with the enemy."

"Shut up. Stormi is not the enemy."

"I think, if you keep following her, pretty soon you will be on a poster."

"We *are* on a poster."

"Not a wanted poster, a missing poster. That's irony number three. You're about to have your picture on two different kinds of posters."

I puffed out air and Stormi rolled, her peaceful face inches from mine.

Arthur doesn't trust you. Sleeping with the enemy.

Did you lead us here?

The door burst open.

"Up! All of you." Both the voice and the face were weathered and husky. "Welcome to the Hive."

CHAPTER 11

The old man disappeared outside, shutting the door behind him.

"The Hive. So, are we bees now? What does that mean?" Arthur spoke to no one in particular.

"Bees work." I stood and stared around the room. I'd not planned well for an extended trip.

Outside of my ill-fated sojourn to the Mayo Clinic, this registered as the longest I'd been away from home. Well, aside from April's Boundary Waters fiasco.

Oddly, the only pleasure trip I'd taken had also sent me north, way north, up through Wisconsin, creeping west to Minnesota, ending a stone's throw from Canada. There, you find the Boundary Waters, aptly named as they form the watery barrier between us and the Canucks.

I had no will to camp, but Ma looked online and located a Boundary Waters expedition specifically for epileptics. Strange, my warped spine had dominated early teen-hood forming the misshapen trajectory of my life and dominating Ma's concern. But when Old Rickety moved upstairs, my back and its limitations were often forgotten. Which is the only excuse I can think of for sending me alongside eight able-bodied campers and a doctor for a ten-day canoe trip.

There was little in Oklahoma to compare to the Boundary Waters. Oh, the Ozarks has its share of lakes and streams, but the sheer volume of water, the pristine quality of the Boundary Waters—you could drink straight from the lakes without worry of amoebas—this was unheard of, and I admit, climbing into the canoe, I thought it: who knew Minnesotans and Canadians had a corner on heaven?

Five minutes in, I discovered that heaven carries a steep price. With a sixty-pound Duluth pack strapped to my twisted back, we prepared for the Grand Portage, a mile-long hike through the forest, during which we'd be hauling all we owned. Our goal was to achieve the next lake.

My fellow campers were an odd collection, bound only by the sickness dormant in our minds. Three girls, two of whom displayed a radiant kind of beauty, were among our number, and pride set in, a disastrous visitor for the feeble.

"Yeah, I can carry a pack and a canoe."

This was the line that did me in. To my credit, I managed for half a mile. Hunched forward, I carried the canoe upside down—an oversize captain's hat concealing my head—stabilized by shaking hands. Aching shoulders felt the weight of the crossbar, but the unusual hunched position provided a strange relief to my lumbar.

At the midpoint I reached a summit, glanced down at a treacherous path, and met Old Rick. He took me at the top, flinging me forward. I do not recall the tumble, and in fact have but flimsy memories of the next two days. That I fell is certain, as Kylie, the prettiest of our group, snapped a photo of me laying face-first at the bottom of the hill, my body eclipsed by canoe, arms stretched out on either side.

Dr. Medroni forced me to sleep in his tent for the remainder of the trip, like a needy child requiring constant observation. From a distance, I witnessed love blossom between four campers. Perhaps it was an appropriate penalty for thinking of other girls beside Stormi. But I returned home feeling less, believing that adventures were not for me.

Still, this trip felt different; I felt different. And not even Arthur's ironic distrust of Stormi could mute that fact. I was leading. Well, maybe leading, while Stormi maybe followed. She had done more than share a tent; she felt at peace in my bed. That had to count for something.

Stormi flattened her hair and straightened wrinkled clothes.

First thing, take my medicine.

Crap.

"I don't have meds, Stormi."

"None?" She paused and looked at me with impatience. "You didn't pack any?"

"Yes, I packed them, but I was hurried out of Gullary, remember?"

"Fine. I'll figure something out," she said, heading toward the small sink. How quickly the girl I held all night could turn.

In truth, seizure meds—items compulsively hoarded back home—were the least of my worries; they didn't work anyway.

However, my lack of fresh clothes felt urgent, as I still smelled faintly of gas. Stormi, too, appeared lost as she washed her face and stared vacantly into the mirror.

A tiny wooden shack, with two windows propped open for ventilation, containing two beds, a toilet, a sink, and a small desk and chair. That is all there was.

Okay, so maybe it is a cell.

"Hurry on, miss." Our wake-up caller reappeared. He sounded tired, though morning was barely upon us. He slipped inside and eased himself down on Arthur's mattress. I didn't imagine there was much hurry left in his aged, arthritic fingers.

Stormi wiped her face and set down the towel. "Ready."

We stepped out into morning, for the first time taking in our surroundings. "Well, we're still in Oklahoma," I said. All year long we'd run fifteen degrees above normal. This was made clear by my skin, not my eyes. The unusual heat came quickly, as it often did in Gullary, but this heat felt different; it was a saturating heat, and I wanted nothing more than to duck back into shade. To the right, Oklahoma stretched out forever, and in this forever, there was a refusal of anything to be hidden. One could see for miles, from the deepest, bluest sky down to the reddish hue of the horizon; it was the uncovering of all things. And I felt uncovered as well.

"The cells are ours, the cabin is yours. Name's Eleven."

A gust of wind swept over our cabin and Eleven raised the red handkerchief from his neck to his face, filtering out the dust.

"Eleven," I repeated, and glanced around the compound. I saw no difference between their cells and our cabin. All identical wooden log construction, with two windows, and large enough for a large man, or two really little ones. Thirty cells surrounded a center courtyard, which boasted only two other buildings.

"Them's the meetin' house, where you'll be eatin' for now," Eleven said, eyeing the direction of my gaze. "And that on the left is the prayin' shed. You won't be goin' in there for any reason." He looked at each of us. "Clear?"

"What if I want to pray?"

Stormi and I turned toward Arthur. It seemed a strange question, as I'd never seen him before at service.

"You won't catch flack for that." Eleven bent over and fisted a handful of reddish dust and threw it into the wind, which drew it back into the sky. "Maybe God'll hear ya. But not in there. Not in *our* prayin' shed."

I had no inclination to pray; this was Ma's territory, and I'd yet to see her prayer on my behalf produce any change to life or limb. I was, however, human, susceptible to all the temptations prohibition brings. Do not go in there? Why not? The shed instantly became the only place here I wished to go.

Eleven winced and shifted his weight. I recognized the maneuver, and felt for him. "Hope you enjoyed your tour, and your sleep-in. Tomorrow I reckon you'll be on detail, but of course that all be up to Q."

"No, we were promised we'd be gone. Any chance we can see Q now?" I asked.

"You will not refer to him by letter. You'll use his name. First and last. And no, not now. He workin' with the men. I's only here as my leg makes me fall behind." He cocked his head, examining me from a different angle. "That back keep you from work?"

"Some, not all." I straightened. "I can do pretty much whatever—"

"Winston told us there'd be nothing asked, nothing required." Stormi interrupted, like I was so much dust. "We need a day or two to sort things out."

"Ain't heard of a Winston, not in here anyways." A swirl of sand up and surrounded us. Arthur and I instinctively lifted our T-shirts to cover our noses, but Stormi stood statued in the dervish, unaffected by the choking swirl. Eleven hawked and spit, squinting through the earth. "What are you sorting, girl?"

The gust moved on. Stormi glanced at me and shook her head, and I read her silencing cue.

Arthur did not. He lowered his shirt and spit, and then blurted, "We're on the run."

Shut up, Arthur!

"Course you are. We all run from something. What you all running from?"

I stepped hard on Arthur's foot, but truth was on a roll.

"Gullary. It's a small town, so you may not have heard of it."

Eleven's face twitched, and he turned a strange shade. He hobbled three steps backward. "Gullary. And how did you come here?"

Arthur shrugged. "By truck." But Eleven didn't bother to listen. He hoofed it toward the prayer shed, took one glance back in our direction, and disappeared.

Stormi stared after him. "How *did* we come here, Jonah?"

Arthur stepped between us. "I think that's your question to answer, Stormi."

We were breaking apart, I felt it. Trust and mistrust fighting it out.

I hung my head, slowly wrung my hands, and Stormi continued. "Or would you like me to ask the ever-truthful Arthur?"

It was so complicated, it didn't matter anymore.

"Okay. The truth as I know it. It was Old Rickety. And then we were locked in and you were so furious and you wanted to get away and I wanted to get away and I wanted you to stop hating me, so I figured you might if you thought I knew a place. Then Arthur gave me this and I had a place to go." I reached in my pocket and brought out the chess piece, turned it over in my fingers. "It seemed as good a place as any. It felt like a mystery. Like maybe I knew something you didn't. For once you didn't know, it was secret between me and Arthur and—"

"Tres," she whispered.

"Tres. But I didn't know he was your grandpa, or that he was out to get us, or that we'd end up on a poster. Honest, it was just someplace to go."

Stormi started to pace. "So we're hiding from Tres in the place Tres wanted us to go."

"Indirectly," I said.

Arthur leaned over and offered his volume-packed whisper. "Technically speaking, it's a direct correlation."

"Thanks, Arthur."

He nodded curtly. "Stormi, Jonah has now told you everything. We wanted to reach Bishop, and Tres wanted us there. My question is, why are we *here*? A lot of this . . ." He gestured dramatically. "It seems to be a result of your doing. I don't think Jonah wanted to follow Winston at all."

I exhaled. "Accusations don't help, Arthur. I'll take it. My fault." I raised my hand. "I picked the town. Didn't know anything about this place. I don't know what I knew, seizures picking up as they are. But no matter how we got here, or who brought us here, we're here, right? We stick together. We stick—"

Stormi stepped toward me as if to strike, her violent Stormi eyes squinting with hate. Two inches from my chest, she took a sharp left and swooshed by me without a word. Even her breeze was pissed. She opened the cabin door, slamming it shut behind her.

Arthur winced. "I think perhaps I caused you some trouble just now and—"

I placed my hand over his mouth. "It's good it came out. From now on, maybe keep your wonderings about Stormi to yourself. Come on." I grabbed his arm and pulled. "We need to be gone long before this Q comes back, but first we're checking that shed."

"But you heard Eleven. It's illegal."

"Aren't you a little bit curious? Why an old man freaked when you mentioned Gullary?" I spun and grabbed both his shoulders, shaking gently. "Why a genius able to place you in zugzwang sent us to this spot?"

Arthur looked back toward the cabin, and when his face returned, it was all smiles. "A genius and his genius grand-daughter. This is Stormi's doing. But, yes, I'm curious."

Stormi exploded out the door, hand extended. "Not funny, Jonah! The truck keys. Now."

"I, uh, don't have your keys."

"They aren't where I left them. How are we supposed to leave if . . ." She froze, eyes frantic. "Give me five minutes." She raced around the side of the cabin.

Arthur and I glanced at each other.

He cleared his throat. "Doesn't that seem a bit odd to you?"

"She's been odd since the day we left. Don't know what that's about, but five minutes is all we need," I said, and walked toward the shed. We reached the door. Arthur turned the knob, and the wooden door swung open with force, catching me square on the kneecap, sending me to the dirt.

"Arthur, you idiot." I started to stand, and froze. There stood Q. I didn't need to be told. He was tall and strong, the muscles in his arms rippling with both power and years. Tanned, bald, and earringed, he looked like a pirate, or like Mr. Clean on Mom's disinfectant.

He stretched out an arm and pulled me to my feet as if I were a child.

"Not for you." He closed the door gently behind him. "My name is Michael Queene, and you may address me as such. Not Michael as my father did, nor Queene as acquaintances do. And though you will hear the men refer to me as Q, it is used only by those who know me well." He looked carefully from me to Arthur and back again. "The Hive functions because we have rules and trust. Do you understand these words?" Q folded his arms, and examined my back. "I asked if, as guests, you understand the importance of both those concepts. Have you not been taught?"

Arthur nodded and folded his hands. I swept the dirt off my jeans.

"My question was simple. Has your schooling not addressed issues of propriety?"

"My ma has . . . Michael Queene, sir," I answered.

"Which then begs the question: Why would you ignore your upbringing and the admonition of your own flesh and blood to do what you should not?"

"I guess I wanted to look."

"You are guessing. Turning a true false into a multiple choice. The command is clear—honor your father and mother that it may go well with you in the land. Why did you disobey your parents?"

His voice was deep and smooth, the kind of voice that places you at ease, even when you're certain you're in danger. Almost hypnotic, it was.

"I guess—"

"Do not begin with a guess, begin with the truth. Why did you choose rebellion over your Ma's instruction?"

"I'm a disobedient child?" I'd not before thought of myself as such, but there seemed little option. Q breathed deeply. "Stand up straight when you speak, posture matters. It communicates confidence."

"I can't."

By now we were so far afield, I no longer wanted anything but to see Stormi. Did I say her name out loud?

"The girl?" Q's voice penetrated.

"We don't know. She ran off," Arthur said.

"I see." Q sighed. "For her own good, I should find her. You should wait in the cabin."

"I think so too," Arthur said.

"Do not think. Let your yes be yes and your no be no. Say what you know, no more. Let's rehearse your sentiment again. You, Michael Queene, should go find her."

"Yes, you Michael Queene, should go find her."

Arthur was gone, trapped by Q's trance, but again the words from Tres's note rattled around inside me, took up residence, broke the spell.

Avoid Q to prevent more loss.

"It's time we leave." I rounded Arthur's shoulder with my arm and started a brisk walk toward the cabin. Michael Queene made no move to follow, watching us from the front of the shed.

"*We* need to find her, and find that Winston, and—"

Ahead, Stormi raced back into the courtyard. "It's bad. I hot-wired the truck. But they've drained the tank. I wired six more. All drained. Not a vehicle in that garage has a spit of gas in it. Jonah? What's happening?"

"I don't know." I turned and pointed at Q, slowly striding our way. "That's Michael Queene—first name, last name, use them both—and he's in charge of this hive, I know that. Be careful of his voice." I stared into Stormi's eyes. "We'll get out of here if we stick together."

I glanced back at Arthur. He was gone, walking quickly back toward Q. Soon, given Arthur's honesty, Q would know all our friend knew, which was pretty much everything.

"We don't leave without Arthur." I exhaled hard. "Agreed?"

Stormi let out a low whistle and drew close to my side. *"Arthurus hypnotizimus?"*

I forced a smile. "Yeah."

Okay Tres, why am I here?

CHAPTER 12

I sat with Stormi in silence. Hours alone in the cabin somehow separated us from each other, from ourselves. My mind floated back to her words, words of affection for me. How I would have soared to hear them in Gullary, but the winds had shifted, and she wasn't the same.

Maybe I wasn't either.

"You think he's all right?" Stormi spoke to nobody in particular. "He's been with that guy for hours."

"I don't reckon Arthur can get in too much trouble."

Outside, the muffled sound of men's voices surrounded the shed, and Stormi and I exchanged glances. "We stay together, no matter what," I said.

"Like we're together now?"

Stormi would never ask that. Not my Stormi, but I got up from Arthur's bed and sat down at her side, and lied. "We're fine."

The door swung open and Winston motioned us outside. "Come on."

I rose quickly and met him at the door. "Why'd you bring us? Why are you keeping us?"

"Keepin' you? You came on your own volition. No force used. Once here, we simply ask you to follow the rules set forth." He spun and strode toward the meeting hall.

"It's okay, Jonah." Stormi joined me, leaning her head against my shoulder. "I kind of freaked back there, but I've been thinking, being here has benefits. I don't think the police will find us. Cartwright won't find us. Tres doesn't seem eager to come, or he would have been here already. It's okay."

We walked hand-in-hand across the dusty ground.

Men streamed silently by us on all sides, either unaware of or uninterested in our presence. They lined up outside the hall. Perfect single file.

"Three, Seven, Eleven . . ."

They shouted numbers as they entered the doorway. "Fifty-two, Fifty-four, Sixty-one."

Stormi and I paused at the threshold, and then followed.

Two rows of picnic tables lined the length of the shadowy room. Three stained glass windows provided what little light there was. Arthur marched up to greet us.

"I'm glad to see you. I'm sorry I left. I told him everything, Jonah. Everything about you and Stormi and Tres. I told him everything. I had to. I'm sorry."

I shook my head. "It's all right."

"Sit." Q's word dropped all but the three of us onto the benches. We stood surrounded, like uncaged zoo animals. Q leaned back, folded his arms. He appeared more than happy; he was thrilled to make us a spectacle, to see us squirm, and

I hated him. I'd been a spectacle my entire life—in Gullary, it was my role. But no longer. Stormi stroked her necklace. She needed me, and here, far from the parents I had disobeyed, I felt a twinge of new, of strength.

I straightened as best I could and glared back at Q.

Stare away. I am Jonah Triumphus.

"Bow your heads."

"I will not bow to you," I whispered.

"Dear Lord," Q began.

Oh.

"Help us know right from wrong. Help us choose right."

The room erupted in unison, "Help us know right from wrong. Help us choose right."

"Amen." Q gestured to three chairs next to him, and soon we were seated, Arthur on his right, Stormi and me on his left.

Men spoke in hushed tones, ignoring us completely, all except for Winston. I caught him glancing our way.

"Jonah, where's Tres?" Q asked.

"I told you we don't know," Arthur interjected, and quickly fell silent.

"Who's Tres?" Stormi asked.

Q took a long drink. "There is a stupidity that comes off as simple ignorance. This is forgivable. Then there is a stupidity that is truly stupid. You, Stormi, are walking the path of the latter."

I cannot express how deeply his words shook me. Stormi had been called unnatural and odd, but nobody questioned her intelligence. She was the smartest one in every room, in control of all that transpired, and we all knew it. All but Michael Queene.

"Jonah, again, I ask you, where's Tres?"

"Who's Tres?" Stormi repeated, reaching for a roll.

How the question irked Q. The muscles around his face tightened, but only for a moment. Later, I would realize the battle Stormi waged here on my behalf, but we rarely understand such wars as they transpire.

Q dabbed his mouth with his napkin. "Are you familiar with King David and his prideful attempt to number his soldiers?"

Of course she wasn't. I knew David had whipped a pebble at a giant, but that was it. Stormi hadn't been to church, well, ever.

Stormi stood up. "I will tell you all a story."

I will not forget the next five minutes. A hall silent, except for Stormi, sharing a tale I'd never heard, of a general named Joab, charged by King David to count David's soldiers, a move which apparently displeased God mightily. So much so that God presented David with one of three calamities as punishment. Door number one: three years of famine. Door number two: three months of fleeing from David's enemies. And door number three: three days of a plague sent from the hand of God himself. David chose the plague, and seventy thousand men gave up the ghost. There likely would have been more casualties, but God held back the hand of one angry angel.

"Three days of plague," Stormi repeated, "that was it—three days. Then God showed mercy. We've been here one day now, after two more I expect to be mercifully released." She cast her terrible Stormi gaze at Q. "I would think you, Michael Queene, a man so bound by Scripture, would attempt to follow the principles found there, wouldn't you?"

Not a soul moved. Stormi sat down, reached for her water glass and took a sip. Q cleared his throat. "Tres's whereabouts are all that matter to me. You are here only until I know."

Stormi's eyes flashed. The space between sky and ground where lightning passes through? That's where I was. "Tres's whereabouts are all that matter to me as well, but I might have a better memory if you told me more about him."

"Have not your parents taught you to respect your elders?" Q regained his footing, and having slipped into his parental obedience quicksand myself, I stepped on Stormi's foot, tried to keep her from moving forth. She'd done so well.

She kicked me. "Orphans aren't taught. Dead people don't teach anything."

Stormi never spoke of her birth parents, except in an occasional stolen letter. Were they dead? Suddenly, I wanted to know.

"You've never been more wrong. I've simply been eager to speak with Tres for some time." Q shifted. "It's my understanding he's been unavailable."

"Not to Jonah." Arthur chose this moment to be Arthur.

I tossed a roll at his head, but Q intercepted it, placed it gently on his own plate.

"Jonah, you really don't know where you are, or why you're here, do you?" Q leaned back. "The Hive runs with precision and order. These two qualities bring my men comfort and some semblance of peace. This is my job, my calling. You can see why visitors may cause needless unease."

"Send us away, then." I leaned forward. "You want to find Tres, we don't. Send us away."

Q smiled. "To a young man, the remedy, of course, seems harmless enough, but you have only a small piece of the picture. I don't blame you. Even old men can be fools."

He glanced to his left, and I let my gaze follow. I blinked hard, and my heartbeat pounded. At a solitary table sat three men. I'd seen them only once, but their faces would not leave me. I knew them without their black suits, without their black hats.

One of them knew me.

I forced a smile. "I sure hope you find Tres soon. You know all we know. May we leave?"

"May we leave," Q repeated. "Perhaps both our desires are best met if you remain with us. Arthur mentioned Tres and Stormi's unique connection. If he's looking for you, it only makes sense that he will eventually come to us, at which point we both have what we want."

"Except that we don't want to see him," I said.

Q stood. "That appears to be inevitable. The question is, do you want to meet that criminal alone, or would it be safest for you here. I think the latter. Good night." He strode toward the door and again the room fell silent. The moment he exited, every man rose, calling his number as he too slipped into the night, which left the three of us alone.

"This Hive of yours is a cult, some kind of freakish place." Stormi slowly wandered to the center of the room. "Michael Queene's the leader, the rest a bunch of worker bees from who knows where." She quieted. "I don't know what's worse. Meeting Tres, or being stuck here."

I nodded, and then frowned. "What do you mean, Hive of mine? I didn't know anything about this place."

"You said you did."

"I said 'I know a place.' Generally, not specifically."

"Tres knew it."

"Technically and semantically, she's got you, Jonah." Arthur nodded.

"Yeah, well, I screwed up, okay? I screwed everything up. But it's not like I'm the only one who's been a little secretive."

"Technically, he's got you there, Stormi."

"Arthur, why don't you ask Jonah how *specifically* he plans on getting us out of here?"

Arthur looked confused. "She wants to know—"

I stood and stared at Stormi. "Tell her I'm working on an ingenious plan as we speak."

Arthur cleared his throat. "Apparently, Jonah is, even as we speak—"

"Tell Jonah that I wouldn't trust his ingenious plan if it was the only ingenious plan in existence."

Arthur opened his mouth and let it fall shut.

"Go on," Stormi said. "Tell him."

"Stormi—"

"Wait!" Stormi stepped forward. "Add in that I am working on my own ingenious plan, so he can give that brain of his a rest."

"Stormi—"

"Wait again."

Arthur sat back and folded his arms.

"Tell him that I still do."

"Your sentence is missing a few needed words, not that you would let me get to them," Arthur said.

I stepped around the table and walked toward Stormi. "You still do? 'Cause I kind of figured stuff changed. At least it felt like it had, or it felt like you had . . ."

"Still here," she said quietly, and stretched out her hand. I took it and drew her near, feeling her softness, suddenly wanting to feel much more.

"You two make absolutely no sense." Arthur shook his head and joined us. "So we're staying then? The food is good. Q seems nice enough."

"No, we're leaving," Stormi spoke into my chest. "Jonah's thinking of an ingenious plan."

She always did know what to say, and her trust kicked me back a few years.

"Wasn't that thing weird today?"

Stormi and I walked home from school, already the best of friends by third grade.

By "that thing," she meant the annual scoliosis screening. Girls visited privately with Nurse Loyna, but not the guys . . . oh no, every guy in Gullary Primary was shipped to the gym, where we stripped from the waist up, pressed our palms and leaned over, as if to touch our toes. A special doctor hired by the district slowly wandered behind our posteriors, staring at our spines. Principal Haynes walked beside him with a clipboard.

"Clear. Clear. Monitor. Clear. Clear."

His voice boomed. I didn't know who received the dreaded "monitor" labels, as I stared upside down back through my legs, but I pitied each one of them. The term *scoliosis* itself sounded terminal.

"Monitor. Clear. Clear." His voice strengthened. The guy was getting nearer. "Clear, Clear. What the—"

His shock occurred directly behind me, and the next thing I knew, he was tracing my lumbar with his thumbs. "Absolutely profound. Why hasn't this been caught?"

Haynes began fumbling about as if my back was a blight on his record. "It won't happen again," he managed.

"What's your name, son?"

"Jonah."

"You may straighten."

I did, and from the other side of the gym, somebody farted. The gym erupted, and several other gas bombs followed. I would have enjoyed it had I not been receiving a death sentence.

"Son, I've not seen a case of scoliosis this marked before. Do your parents know?"

"Am I going to die?" I asked.

"No."

"Then they don't know." I exhaled, thankful that I had caught something that would not lead to death, though right then, Peter Yallis and Riley Trew shuffled away from me. Who knew, scoliosis might be contagious.

I told Stormi about it on the way home.

"Well." She thought for some time. "If you have it, I want it too."

"No, you don't."

"You're the best-looking boy in third grade. Mom says so."

"Ms. P?"

"She's always saying how tall you are. She says how handsome that curly blond hair is. How strong you are."

"Strong? How would she know?"

Stormi looked off. "It's going to rain. We should hurry." She took off running.

"Stormi! Tell me about the strong part."

Yep, how early she knew what I needed to hear.

We slowly walked around the courtyard, Stormi's hand still tucked in mine. In the dark, it wasn't immediately clear which cabin was ours, but familiarity was already setting in, and the three of us quietly approached the door.

"Nobody else is up?"

"There's a curfew. Supper, then bed." Arthur stepped inside first. "Wow, dark in here."

We felt our way forward, plopping onto our beds. "So, tomorrow we figure out how to get out of here."

A voice from the direction of the desk: "You may not have that long."

CHAPTER 13

Some warnings cause the heart to beat with gusto. This warning coupled with a short shriek from Stormi nearly ended me.

I, surprisingly, was first to find a voice, speaking at the shape across the room. "What's going to happen to us?"

"I don't know."

Winston.

"It's the way of the Hive. Everyone knows a part. Keeps all of them from thinking too hard about what's being done."

"I don't understand," I continued.

"If you shoot someone dead to rights, you maybe feel it. But it don't hurt nothing if your job is only to buy bullets."

"And what's your job?" Stormi's voice shook.

"I ain't come to talk about me. I don't have much time before quarters are checked."

"You lied to us." I straightened and winced as my back expressed its displeasure. "You said there'd be nothing required, but we're stuck here now. You said we could leave whenever we wanted to and—"

He pushed his hands through his hair. "Shut up, I know what I said."

167

My eyes became one with the night, and I could see Winston rubbing his temples. Coming back here tonight hadn't been easy.

"Listen." Winston's voice dropped. "They will be coming, maybe tonight, maybe tomorrow night. But I think it's in their nature, so you best be ready."

"They?" whispered Stormi.

"The Hive. All of 'em. Didn't know what I was getting into when I took this job. 'Need a caretaker,' Queene said. 'The old caretaker has passed on and we need some young blood to help the older ones around here.' It was back in '09, and times were tough, so I took it. I took it. Only way I saw to feed my family."

"You have family here?"

"No, I ain't crazy, but they know where I live, where my young ones live. Queene has reminded me of this point several times. You ain't the only one who's as good as trapped." Winston leaned forward. "My job is food runs. Medicine runs. Whatever they need from the outside, that's what I get. Spend the weekends at home, the weeks out here in this accursed place."

"But you brought us here." Here, my naiveté showed bright, but I could not seem to overcome this point. People can be cruel and self-serving; I of all people should have known this.

"I did," Winston continued. "The Drinking Hole is the only business within twenty miles of this place. Queene wants me there, posts me there to listen. If I hear something unusual, he wants to have a look. The man hasn't left this compound for decades, but I reckon he knows more than anyone the ways of the outside."

"You're the eyes and ears, then. The hands and feet. Then you must know why he keeps us." Stormi hugged her arms, while outside the night winds howled.

"No." Winston shook his head. "Though I do know pieces are moving."

"Chess pieces?" Arthur asked.

"Sure, kid. Whatever. Listen, a few days ago, three of 'em came to me at night. Said they had a pass from Q. Said they needed to attend a family event. In short, they needed a ride. I was gassed and ready, so I took 'em to a tiny armpit town the other side of the state."

"Gullary," I said.

"Well, turns out they went without Queene's permission, and hell broke loose when we returned. The Hive turned inside out and Queene almost lost control."

"All because three men went to a funeral?" I asked.

"All because three men returned to Gullary."

The air grew thick. "Returned?"

"Ah, now you see the magnitude of a word. These aren't the first cells the men here in the Hive have occupied. You once had a prison in Gullary, filled with the most heinous humanity could offer. But a storm came, and their bonds broke away. True enough, some probably died beneath the rubble, but most didn't, and them that escaped came here."

Stormi pressed into my side, and Arthur joined us on the bed, breaking all his personal space rules.

I tried to clear my throat, but sound wouldn't come, and I swallowed hard instead. "We're living with rapists and murderers and—"

"Nobody here that's not done something worth being locked up for a lifetime. But credit Queene. He knew these violent inmates couldn't live as free men, at least not right off. He put them to work, gave 'em religion. Gave them a new purpose working in the Hive. Think of him as the new warden. He gives off confidence, demands order. Yeah, Queene looks calm, but he's never been, that's because of your friend Tres."

"Grandpa Tres," Stormi said softly.

"Grandpa?" Winston shook his head. "What a tangled web we weave. From stories pieced together, seems as there's one inmate left alive at storm's end but what refused to run with the rest. He chose to stay in Gullary though escape was offered."

"Grandpa Tres."

"And whatever kept your grandfather there, it's enough to keep Queene up at nights, or so the men whisper."

"But how do you know all this?" I asked. "You just buy the bullets."

"Sometimes, the unforeseen happens. Had a stowaway one weekend. Eighty-eight popped up his head and asked me to drive as far away from here as I could. I did what Queene told me, should that situation arise. We took off, slowly circled around, and I brought him back here, but on the way he told me more than I should know, what that now I'm telling you. About the men. Where they's been. About Tres and Q and—Oh, shoot, I will never forget his face when he saw me pull up to the garage. The sadness, and I didn't know. You got to believe me that I didn't know what they would do to him."

"What . . ." I realized I didn't need to know.

"Yeah, he gone. If the guilty three—that's what they call those that went back to Gullary—if Queene didn't keep them isolated from the others, they'd be gone too. I believe many of them got religion, found peace. But you can't force that. Many are here 'cause they're too scared to leave, but inside they're who they was. The ugly's just baked in a little harder."

"I still don't see why Tres worries anyone." Arthur spoke up. "It's not logical."

The door flew open. "Perhaps a bit too late for my caretaker to be paying my guests a social call."

Q stood in the doorway, large and imposing, and Winston shot up. "I miss my family, miss 'em something terrible. Seeing her about Jen's age, I needed to talk."

"Visiting hours are over." Q turned and vanished, leaving the door open.

Winston leaned over, his lips releasing little more than a breeze. "Go on now. Go."

He too disappeared, closing the door behind him. We huddled together.

"Why would Tres want us here?" I asked. "I don't care what anyone says, I spent time with him. He wouldn't want us dead. Stormi, this would be a really good time to know something that we don't."

"Do you believe him?" she asked quietly.

"Who? Winston? Yeah, I mean, don't you?"

"Didn't it all seem odd, him in here and Q showing up right then? He was so willing to tell us everything, but he's never gone to the authorities? There's the family explanation, but his cover was so thought out."

"It doesn't matter," I said. "If they check the cabins, we can't leave. All we have are a bunch of vehicles without gas."

"Nineteen."

We both looked at Arthur, who turned cheery. "Nineteen. He stores the gas. Thirty keeps the keys."

"How?" I asked.

"I know people think I'm stupid, you think I'm stupid, but didn't Michael Queene make you uncomfortable with that voice? I took it upon myself to find out what he knows, which you two couldn't do sitting in here, I might add."

I'd not felt the desire to kiss a guy before, but the urge overwhelmed and I planted one on his cheek. "You got Q to tell you all that. Ma would call you a blessed child."

Stormi stood and paced. "So we know who has what we need. We don't know which cell they're in. Unless you found that out too."

"No, I didn't. We need to stay awake tonight. One of us all the time." Arthur peeked out the door. "Knowing who's who doesn't help if we're dead. If we make it until morning, we go to work with the men. They yell their numbers on the way in to meals, so we should be able to figure out who the two are. We can track them back to their cells, and the next day when they go off, we grab what we need."

"And none of this goes to Winston, right?" Stormi grew excited. Hope returned to her words.

"Agreed." I sealed the matter, and then paused. "Arthur, I'm not sure what we'd do without you. Sorry for the way I made you feel small and stupid."

"I accept your apology, as long as you take the first watch." He jumped into bed. Stormi slapped my back and did the same, leaving me vertical—well, almost vertical. It could be worse. There was danger all around, but I was held fast by a true friend and a girl I loved.

Loved?

I walked toward the door, my mind fixed on that word, wondering when I should use it. Talk about danger.

CHAPTER 14

I stayed awake all night, my eyes peering out the cracked door and into the darkness. Truth had fallen from Winston's lips—the Hive was peaceful. Hard to fathom some great evil lurking about in the hearts of men, but then again, looks were deceiving. Even Gullary had turned, shifted, become less my home and more a quicksand. We'd only been away a few days, but the tether that had held me fast bound me no more. Now free floating, I could sense how secretive we'd been. Something lay under the surface.

Perhaps every place had its secrets.

My granddad and I crossed but briefly in this life.

Memories of him are light and vapory, more gas than solid. I remember his smell, and the Old Spice aroma that lingered in his car and his home. I remember his chair, brown and mahogany. How I wanted to sit in it. How I was warned not to.

I just can't remember his wife.

My grandmother had lived; the existence of Dad makes that a certainty. According to pieces gleaned from a hundred clipped conversations, she outlived Granddad by a mile. But that was all I knew. To our family, she was shadow. Never mentioned, her nothingness never explained.

Yes, I had asked.

"Sometimes your own kin chooses to vanish." This from Ma, who knelt in our backyard garden. She had glanced both ways before crossing this street.

"Vanish?" I was twelve, and the thought felt adventurous, holding the same terrible intrigue as a kidnapping. "Where is she now?"

Ma buried her trowel and pushed back to a sit. "The definition of vanish means she has disappeared."

"Do you know where she is?"

Ma reflected for a long time. "Ask your father."

From him I received nothing but a condescending smile, as if I had waded into territory too deep for me. Her chapter seemed closed.

Until a letter arrived two years later. Dad assembled Ma and me.

"Jonah, it appears that your grandma passed. The funeral has already been held." I recall him glancing sharply at Ma at this point, but thought nothing of it at the time. "I want you to know about this remarkable woman."

This dramatic 180 continued for months. Dad poured story after story into me, about the great travels of my historic grandma, the awful and tragic search she undertook through Mexico to find a treatment for Granddad's souring mind. She was a hero, Dad said. I should never forget that.

But she never showed the slightest interest in even seeing me, so the whole hero narrative never took. I would have liked to meet her.

"Did she know about my back?" I tapped my spine with the trowel. "Did she know about me?"

Ma adjusted the hose. "It's what she knew that kept her away."

I stayed awake all night.

In the dark of early morning, men bustled, and I carefully closed our cabin door. Time to move. "Stormi, Arthur, get up."

Minutes later we joined the comatose shuffling toward the dining hall, myself eager for a little coffee. Any adrenaline I had acquired from the day before had long since seeped away, and I blinked hard as I entered the building.

Arthur pulled me aside, my body offering little resistance. "You look awful. Why didn't you wake me?"

"I was doing fine until an hour ago." Remembering my family made me tired.

We took our seats at the head table, and neither Q nor any other man questioned us. All present waited in silence and darkness. I heard the prayer, but it did not enter; heard hushed conversation, but did not try to listen. Coffee. I drank coffee until we all rose.

We followed the group out into the courtyard, beyond the prayer shed, and onto a rough, stone-paved path that exited the ring of cells. It was too early to care where we walked; my body moved on caffeine and autopilot. The path quickly widened to a patio, and pulling up to it was a familiar squeal. A school bus hauling a beat-up trailer.

I exchanged hopeful glances with Stormi. Maybe we wouldn't need Arthur's plan, not if there was a gassed-up bus at the ready.

I followed Stormi on board and paused. Winston sat behind the wheel. Whatever crime he committed via his "secret" visit could not have been too heinous, and I doubted him all the more. Winston's hands did not shift on his lap, nor did his gaze stray from straight ahead, and we took the front two seats, Stormi and I backed by Arthur.

Loaded, the bus hissed and lurched forward.

An hour later the sun hinted its arrival and still we jarred onward. It felt doubtful that we were on any sanctioned road, given the lilt of our travel. The bounce and the rock grabbed my senses, pulled them back toward slumber, and when we finally stopped, I was barely coherent.

"Beautiful," Stormi whispered, divoting my side with her elbow.

I forced my eyes open. She was right.

I rose and stepped out into a garden. The sound of rushing water was the first thing I heard, the sudden explosion of trees and flowers the first thing I saw.

"Walk around, kids. See what old men hath wrought." Q's voice was low, but it turned on a dime. "To your stations, men. Tasks are set. Get to!"

Men scrambled and clumped near the trailer, grabbing hoes and shovels, shears and buckets.

"We don't have any clear direction," Arthur said.

Stormi took hold of my arm. "Sure we do. Walk around."

Here, I can only ask that you believe this account, though I'd understand if your faith is worn thin. Had I not seen it, I would not have believed such a place existed, certainly not in the barren of the panhandle.

That sound of water began in the garden's center, where a shallow lake rippled gently in the breeze. Given the hour, it reflected the red of morning. In the middle of that lake grew an island, tiny and perfect, home to nothing but two beautiful fruit trees.

Streams trickled out from the lake in four directions, and along the banks grew plants and flowers unseen in Gullary. Everywhere, the men tended and pruned, sculpted and watered.

The younger men worked the practical garden, alive with grains and vegetables. It was perfect. It was beautiful, and Winston's warnings felt remote.

Wish I had my camera.

We wandered the lakeshore. A rowboat waited, and Stormi nodded toward it.

"You think we can?"

"Once again, a child is thinking. This lack of certitude among the younger generation is concerning." Q stepped out of a thicket, pulled the boat into the water, and climbed aboard, beginning a slow row toward the island. "Do you want to join me, yes or no?"

"Yes," I said, and began walking toward him.

"Don't you *think* that's presumptuous? It's my island."

We watched him row clear out to the middle, climb out onto the tiny spit of land, and set up a rotating chair. From there, Q could spin around and see the entire group; he could monitor every move.

He could eat from the trees.

"This whole place is so bizarre." A hundred feet to our left, four men of near eighty fought with a huge tree, dragging it with fits and gasps toward a pre-dug hole. I started toward them to help, but Stormi grabbed my shoulder.

"I have to," I said. "They're not going to make it. They're busting in the heat, and Q's got it easy. It's not right." I turned to Stormi, who bit her lip.

"We need to get out of here," she said gently.

I broke free, jogged toward the men, and returned five minutes later, back on fire but staring at a vertical oak.

"We will. We will leave," I said while clapping the dirt off my hands, though I lacked conviction. "Of course, bizarre as it is, this garden is beautiful. If there weren't maybe murderers everywhere, I mean, we could live here. Right here."

Stormi sighed. "Describe what you see."

"Well, trees, water, pretty much an oasis. Four rivers, two trees."

"Garden of Eden."

"A bit over the top, Stormi."

"Maybe. Do you believe in the story? The Adam and Eve thing?"

"Ma does, Dad doesn't, so I'll go in fifty-fifty."

Stormi quieted. "Two trees were there. The tree of the knowledge of good and evil, and the tree of life. They ate from the knowledge tree—"

"And figured out they were nude. I remember that part."

Stormi nodded. "At that moment, sin entered this world. At that moment. What do you think would have happened if they ate from the tree of life after that? I'll tell you. They would have lived forever. Horrors committed in secret would have lived forever."

And here, I cannot tell you what came over her. She eased down to her knees, closed her eyes, and a wash of peace fell over her face. She was transfigured, to use the biggest Bible word I know.

She opened her eyes, stood, and breathed deep. I maintain that though she didn't tell me, it was at this moment that she figured it out. She knew what she would one day do.

"Secret horrors can't be allowed to live forever," she said.

"Yeah, well, I don't know about all that God stuff."

Stormi winked, returning in all her glory. "How about us? Do you know anything about us stuff?" She paused. "Say that we were alone. No Arthur, no Tres following, and no Gullary looking . . . If you and I were really a you and me, what would you do first?"

I thought a moment. Maybe it was the scenery, or Stormi's full attention. Maybe it was the urging of Genesis to be fruitful and multiply. "I'd, uh, I'd try, well, after asking, of course, to maybe kiss you. Maybe?"

"And second?"

"It would kind of depend on how the first thing went."

"Let's assume it went well. Very well."

"Huh." I puffed out air. "I don't let myself dwell on those type of moments. I'm not Connor, you know."

Moment lost. As I look back, this may be the most painful of them all.

Stormi bristled. It wasn't until twenty long paces stretched between us that I realized what I had done.

"Stormi, I, I didn't mean to say that. I mean, I shouldn't have brought him up, or to make you think about all that. Crap."

She was gone, gone from sight, and gone from hope.

"Kid, here's your shovel."

Don't need one. I'm digging deep on my own.

I turned, and a bald, fifty-something held out the tool. "Lots of work today. Good that you're here."

"Yeah, well, right now, I need to talk to Stormi before I can do anything else."

"Love waits. Q don't." He grabbed my arm and hauled me into the nearby field. Rich, black dirt gave easily beneath my feet, and I glanced over my shoulder in time to see Stormi reappear behind a clump of trees. She stopped and held my gaze.

"Move, kid. Planters are comin'. We got a hole to dig."

He plunged his shovel into the dirt, and straightened, leaning on the handle. "Your turn."

"So I dig anywhere?"

"No, fool, right there." He nodded downward, and I positioned my feet, bent, and dug out a scoop. My back throbbed.

I was too far away to flash Stormi an I'm-just-a-stupid-guy look, so I set my mind to digging. "What number do I call you?"

He glanced around. "No number while we're in a hole. Saul will do."

Another thrust, and another. Together we dug one foot. Three feet, widening as we dug. Sweat poured down, but I did not stop: Stormi was still watching. Half a day passed and the hole neared five feet deep, and a similar distance around.

"We planting another tree?" I paused, and crumpled, leaning down against the inside of the hole. Saul peeked over the edge and did the same.

"Ain't for us to know." He scratched in the dirt with his fingers, crusted red with Oklahoma earth. "Nothing asked, nothing required, exceptin' to dig." He stared up at the blue sky and sighed.

I leaned forward, silencing the scream of my vertebrae, searching for any question that'd buy me an extra minute before my next scoop. "How long you been here?"

"Long? Since the start. Some days, seems too long. Others, not long enough."

"Do you ever think of leaving?"

Saul's gaze searched me. He was looking for something; I felt it. But he didn't find it, and let his head fall back against the inside of the pit. "Every day, but there's nothing for me out there. Here, I got work to do."

"These holes?"

He scoffed. "Prayer work. Don't expect you to make sense of it."

"In the prayer shed."

Saul rubbed his face, gave the ground some light jabs with his shovel. "Some memories you don't dig up 'lessen you have to." He shifted, his face aging before my eyes. "I was so young, you know, the youngest. A dumb kid like you—no offense. Didn't know it would go down as it did. I don't think anyone really knew." He paused and looked off. "Maybe Q. Maybe Q knew."

"What went down? What happened? Was it in Gullary?"

He waggled his finger, and then gently backhanded my chest. "Sneaky, you are. Get an old man tired and unhinged in the heat." He slowly rose.

"Do you know Tres?"

Saul dropped down quickly to a knee. "Some names you best not say in the Hive. Come on, orders are to go down another foot."

Together we deepened and widened the hole. Moments later, a rope ladder was lowered and we climbed out. Dirty, smelly, but worked. And the work felt good. I felt good.

I followed Saul to the lake, took off my outer clothes and climbed in along with all the others. Arthur was washing some distance away; I didn't see Stormi, but believe me, I looked.

"What happened to you?"

Old fingers reached out and touched my spine. I recoiled. "That's not really your business." He nodded, offered a sympathetic smile and I softened.

"It's, uh, scoliosis. Bad case."

"Sorry, kid. Gotta be a painful way to live."

My eyes burned, and not from sweat. I plunged down beneath the surface. There, tears did come, and in a strange baptism, they were washed away. Some ancient hand had touched me, had compassion on me, and emotion overwhelmed. It came in splashes and waves unrecognizable. Sure, Stormi's hand brought comfort, but I tell you I'd never felt her fingers reach in that deep.

Ma would later say that I felt the touch of God. I don't know about that. I do know these old guys saw me, uncovered, and what they saw caused them to reach out, not run away.

When I finally brought myself to emerge, my wrinkled god was once again scrubbing, while a few nearby men offered sharp nods and safe glances. Yeah, I could live here with Stormi, surrounded by this new mercy. They may have been murderers and rapists, but they didn't violate my condition.

They left my heart intact.

A sudden splash of water struck my eyes, and when I opened them, the lake was spinning.

Not in water. Not . . . here.

I sloshed toward shore, but made it only two steps before Old Rick took me. Bubbles and gasping on the heels of a miracle. Then no more.

I came to in the cabin, dressed in oversized jeans and an undersized T-shirt. Stormi gently stroked my head, her words calming despite her message.

"Your seizures are stronger than they were. They take you longer and more often."

"Yeah."

"You could go . . . you could go back if you wanted to. Your seizures would improve if you did." Her voice quieted. "You belong there. You don't need to stay with me. I'm so sorry I dragged you into this."

"But it was Tres—"

"I don't think Tres cares much about you."

I slipped in and out of consciousness, but when next I woke, Old Rickety had released me. Stormi hadn't.

"I'm not going back. Not now." I winced my back into a different position. "I just got good at diggin' a hole. What'd you do today?"

"Nothing. But I stayed near you." She lowered her voice. "There's something disturbing here, even more than we were told. We shouldn't separate."

I thought about the hole, the kindness shown me in the lake. "Friendliest place I've ever been." I propped myself on an elbow. "Arthur, what'd they have you do?"

"Builder. They called me a builder." He raised his hand and showed off his callous. "It was basic, simple assembly-line organization. Choppers, planers, followed by builders. Guys chopped down a few trees. Others planed them into rough boards. Builders assembled and nailed the boards together into a crate."

Stormi bit her lip. "How big was your crate?"

"Big enough to lie down in."

"You built a coffin, Arthur." Stormi rubbed her forearms. "And Jonah, you dug the hole. What did you think was going to be planted there, a twenty-foot turnip?"

"I'm no gravedigger." I shook my head. "If that's what we were doing, Saul would have told me."

"If he knew," said Stormi.

Right. If he knew.

"Let's assume Stormi's right." Arthur scratched his head. "It would be logical that someone is going in the crate. Someone's going in the ground. It could be me. I pried information from Michael Queene."

"Or me." Stormi folded her hands. "It's me Tres is after."

"Or me."

I didn't really think it would be me. There was no reason to stick me in the hole, but it seemed the right thing to say.

We sat and thought in silence, until Stormi and I exchanged glances, and spoke in unison. "Winston."

"They have no need to get rid of us." Stormi stood. "We're the bait for Tres."

"Tres doesn't know if we're dead or not," I offered.

Stormi raised her eyebrows. "Doesn't he? He's coming. We need to leave. Tonight. Jonah, while you slept off your seizure, Arthur went to dinner. He knows which cell holds the keys. He knows where the gas is. We leave tonight."

Plans were changing so quickly. Besides, they didn't have all my information.

"Wait. There's another old guy here who touched my back, and I'm telling you neither Saul or him or the others at the lake would, well, they wouldn't hurt anyone!" I was suddenly furious, and took a deep breath. "The wrinkled one he . . . sort of changed me."

Stormi took my hand. "You're doing it again. You believe everything you hear or experience. You think the best of everyone. Snap out of it and assume the worst, please, for us."

"Don't fight. Let me collect what we need," Arthur said. "Jonah, upon further thought, it's my fault we're out here. I let Tres out of SMX. He's the one causing you all this trouble. I did that."

I shook my head, still stinging from Stormi.

"I'll see you soon with what we need." Arthur slowly slipped from the room.

"Where are you?" Stormi looked betrayed, her eyes holding less for me. "Still with me?"

"I'm sure I'm too naïve to answer that."

I, too, slipped out, powered by anger. So I trusted people. What was wrong with that? I paced a bit, slowing at the sight of the prayer shed. It had been taunting me since our arrival, since Q had denied me entrance.

For the first time, I moved through the compound without fear. Purpose gives a guy courage, and I reached the door and ducked inside.

Candlelight lit the room, a space large, simple, and without focus. The room presented no front or back. Church pews filled the shed, facing outward, worshiping each of the four walls. And on those walls, displayed in poster-sized frames, were photos. Pictures of teens. My-aged teens. Guys and girls.

Beneath each photo was a table, on which lay one knife, one bowl, and a towel. I marched right, and stopped in front of an especially beautiful girl, one I swore I'd seen before.

"You almost look Stormi-ish."

Behind me, the door creaked, and I dropped to the floor, crawling awkwardly beneath a pew. There I tried to straighten—to become parallel with the bench—as they provided little cover, but my hunch prevented me. Footsteps, slow and heavy, moved toward the far end of the room. Oak creaked, and I rolled over and sat up, my sight line skimming the top of the backrests. Even from behind, I knew the shape well.

I'd spent the day with him in a hole.

I relaxed. Saul was a friend. All day he showed kindness, certainly contrition. I thought to stand and join him. Then the sound started. Deep and sorrowful and filled with pain. A sob; he was sobbing. It wasn't a sob I had entertained in my life. This one came from a place I didn't know, and never wanted to visit. It was a sob from hell.

For ten minutes, it shook him, and it felt I was invading a moment not made for me. I could run out, but that would be more intrusive, so I grimaced my spine into a crouch and waited and watched, my eyes growing big.

Saul finally moved toward the table, pausing to glance at the girl he fronted, whose confident face smiled down upon him. He grabbed his sleeve, rolled it up to the elbow, and reached for the knife. He cut himself slowly, deeply, the blade moving easily through his fleshy forearm. I couldn't watch. I wanted him to stop, and my fingers clawed the bench.

He glanced up again, and in the soft glow of the candle, crimson dripped down his arm and into the bowl.

What is this place?

Finally, he took hold of the towel and applied pressure to his fresh wound. He stood, let his gaze rise to heaven and prayed, before shuffling toward the door and vanishing. I didn't dare stand, not for many minutes. But I could not remain; Arthur's plan was in motion. He and Stormi would likely be waiting on me. I finally rose and slipped out, bursting to tell Stormi what I saw, hoping she could make sense of something.

I made it halfway to the cabin, and heard more footsteps behind me. Arthur was running, a metal gas can clutched tight.

"Here!" He pressed the can into my gut and jammed a set of twenty keys into my hand. "One of these should start one of the cars parked in front. There's not enough gas in there to get far. I need to find where he stores the rest."

I'd not seen Arthur panicked before. The sight set my heart thumping. "Well, you'll never guess what I saw in the prayer shed. Saul, blood-letting in front of a girl, or a photo of a girl, I mean, there were a whole bunch—"

"Go, Jonah! Stormi's in the garage." He shoved me and raced back the way he came, quietly entering the cell across the courtyard from ours. My mind spun, caught hold of something solid, and I dashed toward Stormi.

She stood outside the garage, all doors gaping behind her.

"He did it?" Her eyes lit, and I handed her the gas can. She gave it a shake, and slumped. "There's not enough here."

"I know. He's getting more. But I have news too." I handed her the key ring. "Wait, how do you know which key goes to which?"

Stormi let her digits stroke the keys' notches, as old Mr. Fredricks had run fingers over his Braille books. She paused on a key. "Caddy. This is an old Caddy." She snaked through the garage, stopping at a rusted Cadillac parked in the front row. "This one. This one here. Fill it."

"But what if it doesn't—"

"It's parked in front. I know the key. Better idea?"

I didn't move.

"Fill it."

I popped the gas door and let a trickle ooze into the tank. Half spilled onto the ground, but I didn't tell Stormi.

"There's even less here than I thought," I called.

Stormi hopped out of the car. "We need Arthur. He'll bring more. He'll bring—"

Last July 4, Jimmy Kleinman waltzed over to his pyro-technic display and flicked his cigarette lighter. Gullary's designated fireworks man, his shows were large and unique, drawing folks all the way from Hinman to the spectacle.

But the last explosions of the night—the grand finale—did not take place hundreds of feet up, as desired. Nope, they blew right there on the ground with a shake that felt atomic to those of us gathered fifty feet away. The first fireball set off others, and folks screamed as the ground shook. Jimmy was not hurt, and local conversation rewrote the ending as the best finale ever.

The explosion that rocked the garage felt like that.

"Arthur!" I dropped my gas can and sprinted back into the compound, Stormi at my side. Men stumbled about, dazed, their faces glowing orange in the fireball that burned on the far side.

The cell Arthur had entered was engulfed, as were the adjacent ones.

"No," I whispered. "That was where he was!" I pointed. "He went in there!" Stormi shook and grabbed me by the arm. "This is our only chance."

I did not move.

"He's gone." She hugged me quick and hard. "He's gone for nothing if we don't get out."

"There's nothing left." My mind spun. "He was right here, talking to me. Just like back home on the bus. Gina was right there, and then she wasn't and now he isn't."

It makes little sense now, what I said and the hesitance I displayed, but explosions steal a mind's rational thought.

"I need you to snap out of this *now*!" Stormi yanked hard and I stumbled, falling backward toward freedom. "Maybe he made it out. Maybe he wasn't inside." I grabbed Stormi by the shoulder. "We said we wouldn't leave here without him!"

"There is no him to leave with!"

From behind the meeting room, Q appeared. "Water! Get water. Douse the houses on the west side! Douse, you fools!" His shocked gaze caught us, and he broke into a run.

"Come on!" Stormi shouted, and we turned our backs on our friend, my friend.

We jumped inside the Caddy, and Stormi fluttered the gas, the engine sputtering.

"God, now would be a really good time to show up," she hissed, and fluttered it again. The engine wheezed and coughed, and beneath her coaxing, roared to life. Stormi eased out, in front of a gasping Q, who slapped our trunk. With a near empty tank, conservation was more important than speed.

"He's dead." My own voice sounded far away.

Stormi checked her rearview and flicked the gas light on the console. "He knew it might happen."

"Did he tell you?"

"I just knew."

I glanced at Stormi. She knew and she let him go. She stopped the bus in Gullary, but let Arthur race to his death. How little I understood the ways of prophets.

CHAPTER 15

Echoes of the explosion played over in my mind.

The panic of our escape subsided, and was replaced by a sickening sense that I was the reason Arthur was no more. It was our friendship, not his and Stormi's, that drew him to his death, and I closed my eyes and saw his parents.

Arthur's dad was the tax guy in town, punching out numbers and pushing up glasses with oversized frames. He worked late into the night, every night, even on Christmas Eve. He was a joke in Gullary, his work ethic simultaneously appreciated and mocked.

He would be up now. Pushing his pencil and clattering his keys. Did he feel it? Did he feel a sudden hole in his world? Likely not. He probably readjusted those rims and kept on working.

"Arthur's dead," I said quietly.

Stormi peeked nervously in the rearview. "Yeah, a lot of people die."

How harsh the comment sounded, hanging all uncaring-like between us. Who was this girl?

"But not a lot of them are my friends."

Stormi's shoulders sagged, and she sighed. "I'll feel it soon. I will. I promise. It's just that right now, I need us to get as far away as possible."

The Cadillac was thankful for the sip, rewarding us with far more miles than I thought possible, but eventually it coughed and lurched. Once, and again.

"That's it." Stormi pounded the wheel and leaned back, gravel crackling beneath the last spin of rubber. "That's it."

We crunched to a stop. Far in the distance, a speck of light. The bar.

"Come on, Jonah. This is where we walk."

We left our getaway vehicle with the keys in the ignition, and moved awkwardly through the darkness. We weren't alone. The yowl of coyotes filled the night, and our pace quickened. But we had a beacon; how powerful was that one pinprick of light, drawing us forward.

Our conversation fell in staccato bursts.

"There are shrines back there," I said.

"Probably. It's like I told you, it's like a cult."

"Shrines to a bunch of teens."

Stormi thought a moment. "Probably teens like us that Winston brought in."

"I don't know. It doesn't matter now. Stormi, what do you want to do once we reach the place? Where do we go next?" My eyes grew suddenly heavy. "Arthur's parents, we need to tell them."

"We can call."

Stormi hummed, softly and peacefully. I thought of home, of Mom and Dad, and of Gullary. I missed it—no, not true. I missed what it was before. When Gina and Arthur were alive, and dreams of Stormi were only dreams, comfortable and out of reach. Now I felt like one of Tres's chess pieces, always moving, playing a game where kids die, Stormi could be mine, and my family was a memory. I felt older, stretched, unsettled.

Noise from the bar reached our ears. Little had changed. The explosion that rocked our ears must not have reached this oasis, though the flatness of earth made me wonder how it could have been missed. Cars roared and people shouted, maybe the same people as before, unaware that my friend was now dead.

We reached the crowd and again pushed inside. The bartender glanced up quickly and swore. "I did not think I'd be seein' you again." He glanced over our shoulder and toward the door. "There was three of ya, wasn't there?"

"Arthur," I said. "There was an acc—"

Stormi stepped hard on my foot. "He went home another way."

"Home, huh? You still have one? Then you best leave and you best leave now. Distance is your friend."

Stormi hung her shoulders. "We have no car, no truck."

"Then you're in a heap." He glanced at her sideways. "Unless you got something else you'd part with."

Stormi closed her eyes and reached beneath her top. "This." She stroked the gold necklace. "Can you help us?"

How willing she was to part with my gift. I shouldn't have been affected. My gut shouldn't have turned. Not after Arthur. Besides, the stupid thing was from Tres, and I was only the messenger. But, shoot, I *was* the messenger. It had come from my hand.

"I gave you that," I said softly.

"I'm listening now." The bartender held out his hand.

Stormi turned to me, but did not risk my gaze. "Take it off. Please. What else do we have?"

I slowly swept up her hair and fumbled with the clasp. Clumsy fingers finally achieved the goal, and I held it up before Stormi. She took hold and gently lay it on the bar.

He picked it up, turned it over in his hand. "Where'd it come from?"

That didn't follow as being important. "Probably a jewelry store," I muttered.

"I'm talking about the who of it. Who gave this to you?" He peered at Stormi, who pointed at me, and I winced.

"All right, um. It came from a guy I knew. A guy who wanted to share something with his granddaughter." I lowered my head. "Name's Tres, if you need to know."

"Tres." He slammed it down. "Nope. I won't take this. Don't want nothin' to do with this. Take it on out."

Stormi's face reddened; gone was any desire to hold on to the gift. Clearly she was deciding how mad to get. Fortunately, we had other problems to deal with. "We need transportation, and this must be worth—"

"More than you know." He lowered his voice and pushed the necklace toward me. I slipped it into my pocket.

We stood there, lost, stuck. I must have looked the part, as a minute passed and the bartender rolled his eyes and drummed his fingers.

"Fine. You didn't walk here," he continued. "What happened?"

"Our car is sitting in the road, out of gas."

"Make?"

"It's a Cadillac," Stormi said. "Low miles. New timing belt. They go first on those engines."

He looked off, dug in his pocket, and slammed down a set of keys. "Rusty Chevy truck parked around back. Old as the hills, but twice as tough. You take it. You'll need it. I'll have one of my guys outside pick up your ride. Keys in the ignition?"

"Yeah, thank you," I grabbed the keys. "Why are you help-ing like this? You don't know our names. I don't know yours."

The bartender closed his eyes. "Fourteen. For years, my name was Fourteen. You ain't the only ones to make it out. And if anyone else does, I'll be here."

We backed toward the door. Stormi wanted to leave, was trying to—I could see her tensing—but she lost her fight.

"What do you know about Tres, anyway?" she asked.

Fourteen broke into a broad smile. "Most honorable man I've ever met. And the angriest. I expect him to be back around soon. I'll tell him you passed through."

"Rather you didn't," Stormi said. And she was gone.

Fourteen chuckled. "She can't run forever, kid."

"How do you know all this?"

Fourteen picked up his paper and settled into his seat. "I'm a bartender. You hear quite a bit. That, and Tres was here not five hours before you came through the first time. Good man. On a mission, I'd say."

I turned and joined Stormi behind the bar. Who was this Tres? A nobody? That was the line in Gullary. A petty thief. One to pity, according to Mom. One to fear, according to Q and Stormi. One to respect, according to Fourteen.

I remembered all the days I treated him like a chore, as though he was hardly human.

"Keys." Stormi softened. "It's just us. Like I planned it. The road and us. A new vehicle the police won't be chasing. Tres likely thrown off our scent." She reached for the keys. "We might have our lives back."

"No. We'll never have them back," I muttered. "They've been purchased, right? Arthur, maybe Winston soon, once Q has his way. Our lives are worth more. They have to be."

We drove into the night, reached the highway, and Stormi soon took the fork north into Kansas. North felt broad and open, and with every mile, Stormi relaxed.

Maybe my Stormi.

That night I dreamed of Stormi, road trips, and the curves of each.

Unlike most journeys through the subconscious, the dream stuck with me into morning, plastered a goofy smile onto my face all day. The particulars will remain mine alone, but suffice it to say that it was filled with words of affection and melodramatic moments. We swore our devotion to each other, 'til death do us part.

'Til death do us part. It's an overused phrase, until death actually touches you.

Stormi tapped my leg. "Wake up. We'll stop here."

I worked my body upward. "Here?"

Morning had not come, and somewhere in the expanse that is western Kansas, guided by stars or gift, Stormi had turned off the highway and then turned again. She had found "here."

"We'll be safe for the night." She eased into a cleared expanse between fields. "Tomorrow, we can choose where to go, who to be."

"Given limited resources, I think I'll stay me." I lowered my window and listened to the sound of wheat rustling around us. Pushing out, I wandered the clearing, the unnatural clearing. There should have been a field here.

"This place feel off to you?" I called.

"It's over here, Jonah. Go turn on the headlamps."

Stormi's voice was caught up by the wind, but her form stood not far in the distance. I ducked inside the truck, did as instructed, and joined her.

She stood frozen in front of a cement cauldron. It was circular and massive, maybe fifty feet across, and who knew how deep.

Inside, in heaps and shadows, thousands of objects. Broken plastic and glass, twisted metal and a tennis ball, and thousands of things hid by the night. I glanced at Stormi, who nodded at the plaque on the cement:

WINDROW, KANSAS
May 23, 1998 Population: 410
May 24, 1998 Population: 0
Here we gathered after the storm.
Here we gathered all that we lost,
and moved on.

"I've heard of these. It's a storm cemetery. A tornado hit right here and the whole town took off." I glanced around. Four wooden structures stood nearby, bent with the weather, bent like me. A house, a garage, a silo, and a shed.

"Must have been a scary night," I whispered, recalling the images on the SMX museum's walls.

Stormi walked back to the truck and soon we stood in darkness. She returned and took my hand. "I think it was. For tonight, what do you pick—house or garage?"

I'd seen too many horror movies. "Garage. Unless it's filled with pitchforks and stuff, then the house."

The side door creaked open and we entered. The moon shone through where glass had been, and in its light I found a smooth stretch of ground, and lay down in the dirt. My back slowly loosened, and I found comfortable. Stormi shifted and rolled. Shifted and rolled. I found another dream, one where the darkness around me vanished into light, and a scream announced the breaking of dawn. I sat up quickly.

"Jonah. And hello, Stormi. It's been some time."

Tres wandered around the perimeter of the garage, pausing to peek out the cracks in the wall.

"Tres." I rubbed my eyes, trying to make sense of where we were, how the three of us found each other. "Are people out looking for you too?"

"No, Jonah, I done served my time long ago. I served it and then some."

Stormi pressed into me, her hand squeezing my thigh. "What do you want?"

Tres knelt on the ground and scribbled in the dirt before taking a seat. He reclined against the wall, resting forearms on his knees. "Guess I be wanting a lot of things."

"Arthur's dead," I said, and Tres's gaze shot up.

"Arthur, my chess friend. That is unfortunate. I'm sorry, Jonah." Tres shook his head. "That . . . I did not see that coming."

I knew I was supposed to be afraid of him—Stormi sure was—but his were the first comforting words I'd heard since the old guy from the Hive touched my back.

"Well, I'll get right to the wanting question, but first I need to tell you a story." Tres let his head thump back against the wall. "You two like stories?"

No and yes, Stormi and I answered simultaneously.

"This tale begins decades ago, with a man named Everett— Jonah Everett the first."

"My granddad."

"The same. Now shut up." He reached in his pocket and lit a cigarette, exhaling long and slow. "Your grandpa, the mayor of your fine town, grew sick and tired of all us miners and our rascally ways. Too much drinkin' and carousin' for his liking, too much petty theft in Gullary. So he and the town council, the Circle they was called, took matters into their own hands. They sectioned off a portion of the town jail for us 'petty offenders.' No trial, no judge. The Circle held folks as they saw fit."

"I always thought that was illegal," I said.

"Illegal don't always mean ineffective," Tres continued. "Gullary tilted crime free. And then the mines closed, most moved on, and there wasn't none left to commit crime. That's when SMX was built, and suddenly Gullary had all the criminals it could handle, safely locked away. Jobs returned, people returned, but so did petty crime, and your grandpa knew what to do. He grabbed a bucket of paint and smeared it crimson on a door. And the Circle begun again, stickin' good folks in SMX for a night."

"That's where you were."

"Two nights, that was my penalty for drunken conduct. Now, admittedly, drunk I was."

I struggled to wrap my head around the possibility. "*My* granddad threw *you* in there."

"He did, and the next night he threw in eighteen more. An underage drinking party. Probably purposed to fill 'm with the fear of God. Eighteen kids, in the cell right by mine."

"The big one. The foul one," I said.

"Yeah."

The night grew cold, and Stormi felt far away, though she pressed harder into my chest. It was Tres and me.

"I don't know how they got into the cell. How twenty hardened criminals broke free from the secure unit and got into our unmonitored wing, but they did. And the things done to those kids. I could hear it. Every cry. Every scream . . ."

So could I. I'd heard the screams mid-seizure.

"They killed them all. The senior class of Gullary vanished that day."

We sat for a while in the truth, a horror that filled in so many pieces, I didn't question it. Stormi didn't either.

"You'd think that justice would follow quick and sure, but guilt does strange things to a town," Tres continued. "Your grandpa convinced the Circle, the town, that every resident would be punished for the crime. And maybe he was right, as they all knew about the red door. He told the town that if the outside found out what'd been done, all would be held responsible, SMX would be closed, and their jobs would again disappear. The pressure to keep silent was great, especially from those who didn't lose nobody, and so the secret held, bound up inside Gullary."

"But you, you could have spoken. You heard it all," Stormi finally spoke, her voice vacant.

"Nobody would've heard me. Jonah the First done realized what I knew, and my punishment for drunkenness commuted from two days to a life sentence."

"No." I shook my head. The urge to protect your kin runs deep, and though I had no reason to doubt Tres, my objection spewed forth. "Granddad wouldn't have done that."

"Oh, it gets worse. When your dad took over, he left the system in place. He knows what transpired as well, son. I'm sorry, but your dad knows everything. He knows Cartwrights done lost a kid. Pickerings lost a kid. And he sure as hell knows he lost a daughter."

I flopped onto my back, staring up at rafters. Breath came shallow. A daughter. My sister. And my jaw tightened.

A monster. I'd always considered myself to be the family creature, hideous in form. I suddenly could not remain still and jumped up, because if true, if Tres told the truth, a more sinister monster roamed our trailer.

"I have a sister? Had a sister?" And here I asked the stupidest question I've ever heard, but grief dulls the mind. "Does my ma know?"

"I'm sorry, son. I am so sorry." Tres sounded like he cared, but he'd been sitting on this for months.

I rose and approached.

"Sit down, Jonah," Tres said.

I kept walking.

"Jonah, sit down."

"No. Not this time. You knew. This whole time I'm giving you food off my table, you knew I once had a sister and my dad knew I had a sister, and you just, you just . . . Screw you, Tres! Screw you!"

"How dare you question me, you arrogant child!" He rose, and we stood, pain to pain. But I couldn't hold it, my heart throbbed and I couldn't hold it. I no longer trusted anybody—not Stormi, not family, not Tres—and my legs buckled. Stormi eased me back to a sit, and minutes later, Tres too eased himself down.

We sat in silence. "Who were they?" Stormi asked. "The kids. Do you remember all their names?"

Tres stared at me. "You'll forgive me for not caring too much about Evangeline, your sister. Your dad has stolen my years, my life!" He rubbed his face hard. "I only think on one. Lanie. Her name was Lanie. And she was beautiful." Tres swallowed. "And she was mine."

"Your daughter?" Stormi asked.

He stiffened. "My girl. A man should never hear the sound of his girl being . . ." Tres cleared his throat. "So I sat and I waited for justice to fall, and it did. The storm came. Odd, the form 'justice' takes. Those that committed the crime survived. You met three of them at Gina's funeral. The rest, you probably encountered in the Hive. The twister threw open an escape hole and I stood, staring out at freedom, but I couldn't leave, couldn't throw my hat in with 'm, 'cause I heard their voices while they did what they did, and 'cause I knew help was comin' to Gullary." He looked sharply at Stormi. "A truth teller like me."

Tres shuffled in front of Stormi. "Why do you think you're here? Right here. Blind luck?"

Stormi had atrophied on the spot, like so much petrified wood.

"You drove, I'll bet. And you drove here. Well, welcome home. Windrow, it's where you was born. Born to my precious other daughter. Becky. Your mom's name. Died in the storm here, the same one that took Gullary, but you was spared. Spared for a specific purpose, I believe. To expose what'd been done, what's been hidden by the Circle. The Jonah Circle. That was your job in Gullary. You familiar with Exodus 20:5? Read up. But love for Jonah done blinded you. You was blinded by the pain you would cause Jonah if he knew, knew what his family was, and is."

"Love?" I asked.

"Shut up," Tres said. "It became clear Stormi needed a push. Consider this your push."

"What do you want me to do?" Stormi sounded small.

"Unearth what's been buried. Do right by all the kids, by my daughter. By your aunt. Nobody'll listen to a criminal, but you, if you go back and say what's been done, we'll see true justice fall."

"You really are my grandpa?"

"Sorry, darlin'. You don't get to choose family." He scooted back. "You also don't get to choose your gifts. You can see a little before, you can *see*. It was in your mother, which is why she left that God-forsaken town. It's in me." His face softened. "Which is the only reason I could best that Arthur in chess."

"The letters. The two halves that fit!" I said.

"Yeah, I could see hers, see the words, the shape. She likely could have seen mine, if she would've let herself."

Stormi shifted around, her back toward Tres. For minutes she sat in silence. When she spoke, I could barely make out her words.

"What if I don't return? What if Jonah and I move on?"

Tres stood, his voice terrible. "Then Jonah will never see his family again."

"I have no family," I hissed.

Tres paused. "I figured you'd say that. And hate me if you want, but I'm the only one telling you the truth. If Stormi don't go back, you'll die."

I felt a wallop of heat and light and the world spun. There was no aura, no warning that Old Rickety was here. He suddenly was, and in a moment, I wasn't.

I woke beside Stormi.

But she wasn't actually beside me. Always, her hands soothed me as Old Rick departed. Not this time. She sat, now her back turned to me, her hands in her lap.

"Stor, Stormi?"

She didn't answer.

My gaze flitted around the garage. "Where is he?"

"He blew out the way he came."

"Did I dream him? Did we both dream him?"

"No." She stroked her necklace, the one that should've been in my pocket. "Do you know where you got this?"

I closed my eyes. "I told you. Tres."

"He bought it for his Lanie, one day before. He was going to give it to her. He wanted me to have it."

"We don't have to go back," I said. "Old Rick isn't so bad."

Stormi swore, the first and last time I ever heard her do so. "I hate loving you."

CHAPTER 16

I woke with Stormi's words filling my thoughts, and I slowly rose, brushing myself off.

"Stormi?" I peeked out a crack in the wall, and my stomach sank. "Stormi!"

I ran outside, and slowed, my heartbeat finding its proper rhythm.

She was leaned over the cement wall, reaching for junk and setting the pieces on the concrete ledge.

I wandered to her side, but she did not slow.

"Whatcha up to?"

"I lived here." She retrieved a baby rattle, stared at it, then tossed it back. "When this happened, this was my home."

"Technically, you had blown away by the time they built this."

Stormi paused long enough to deliver a potent scowl.

"But yeah, I mean, you were here." I picked up one of her salvaged items, a musty book jacket. *Gone with the Wind.*

"Appropriate," I said.

"Why?" she asked. "Why do you think that's appropriate?"

"Well, the title and all."

"Ever read it?"

I shrugged. "Not all of it. I saw the movie."

"Scarlet's afraid to do what she must. To save what she loves, she thinks she'll lose herself."

"And that's you?"

"I think I lost myself long ago. I think I've been running from myself and I finally caught up. I need to go back."

I turned and walked back to the truck, and hopped inside. It would be a disaster to return. If half of what Tres said was true, an absolute disaster. All the guilt for Gina, for Tres's escape, and certainly Arthur's death, all of it would land on her. And I would be complicit. Dad and Ma wouldn't consider me involved in the diabolical, but I would be pegged as a mesmerized poodle, panting after Stormi and assisting her evil plans.

Yep, that would be me.

Here, far from Gullary, the seizures were intensifying, increasing in number, but I felt myself. As if I had control of myself, and it felt good. Plus, she said love. Or Tres said love and she didn't correct him. No, she had said it. She loved me. I loved her.

Away from Gullary, we loved each other.

I had no guarantees if we returned.

In time, Stormi joined me. "You understand why I can't stay here."

"Yeah, not here, but not Gullary either. I don't understand why you would think of going back to Connor and Ms. P and a bunch of people who think you're responsible for everything."

"Maybe I am."

I reached up and grabbed her hand. "You aren't." I sighed. "Listen, how about you give me a day? We don't talk about Gullary. We don't talk about Tres or Arthur. We live, we just live for a day. At the end, if you still want to go, we will."

I kissed her hand. "Give me one day."

Her gaze traveled from her hand to my eyes. "One day."

"It's only one day."

Ma picked me up from school and drove to the bus depot. At thirteen, my back had begun its most profound shift, and she was concerned, no, terrified.

"The International Scoliosis Association puts these camps on all over the country. You'll make friends. You'll feel normal."

Translated: You're such a loser.

When I arrived, a man bent beyond belief met me at the bus stop, offered a condescending smile, and herded me toward his car. Two other cottonwoods hunched in back, staring downward.

I slipped in the front and straightened as best I could, to prove I wasn't like them, that I didn't belong in this car or at this camp. To my discredit, I spent the entire next day ranking the angles of other kids' backs. By the time I left, I had assigned 101 kids a number. Me, I was 101.

I returned triumphant. I had seen how miserable others looked, and it made me feel good.

I ran over to Stormi's as soon as I got home. We went for a bike ride, and I told her about all the twisted, deformed kids at camp.

"Were you kind to them?"

Stormi sounded like Ma.

"I wasn't anything. Those kids are way bent. They're not like me."

Stormi let go of a handlebar, reached over, and stroked my back. My, she looked sad. At the time, I thought nothing of it, but already, she knew.

We drove into Harmony, Kansas, beneath a bluer sky.

Sure, it was all a ruse, a game, a trick to forget all that awaited us, but the fantasy took hold, likely because we wanted it to. We both wanted it to so badly.

"We should get married." Stormi glanced over, wild-eyed.

"Us? When? Wait, what? You actually want to?"

"More than I can say." She slowed the truck. "Do you?"

Well, shoot. I'd visited every situation pleasurable to a hormone-filled guy. But marriage, that lay in a different universe.

"I guess, someday."

"You guess? That's all the conviction you have?"

"No, Stormi, I can muster more, but leaping into marriage with me?" We pulled up in front of the post office. "Seems a tiny bit . . . monumental."

"I always knew we would." Storm leaned over and kissed my cheek, long and deep and real. Shivers visited the embarrassing parts, and I shifted in my seat.

"Come on." Her eyes twinkled. "Let's send our invitations."

We hopped out and Stormi took my hand and pushed into the post office. She pulled me to the counter, grabbed a few blank sheets from the recycle bin, and handed me a pen.

"Okay, we each should send one invitation. Who would you invite?"

I thought a moment. "My lying folks, I guess."

Stormi exhaled. "I'd invite Connor, so he could see it. Write to your folks. Tell them we eloped and got married."

"But we didn't."

"Now you're sounding like Arthur—" She paused and exhaled. "I'm sorry. I'm sorry. You can untell them tomorrow, but today, we celebrate."

I stared at my blank sheet.

Ma, Dad. I'm getting hitched. I'm getting married to Stormi, because I love her and she loves me, and I'm not some monstrous eunuch. Inside, I burned. *So you screwed up. You treated me like a castrated child, but you turned out dead wrong and now this is what you get, a prophetess for a daughter-in-law, and she knows everything you do.*

I dropped my pen. I could have kept going, but I didn't want them to spoil my engagement day.

Behind me, Stormi leaned over the counter, returning with two envelopes complete with licked stamps. She took my letter from the counter and inserted it without so much as glancing. She scribbled an address, and I watched my rage drop into the mail slot.

We exited and Stormi stretched. "We can't find a justice of the peace on such short notice, but we can skip that and get to the enjoyable part."

At this, I tell you my body trembled with a severe joy. What type of anticipation does this statement bring? Her and I. Us, together.

"Uh." My voice tripped over itself. "Where should we, you know?"

Stormi glanced around, and then pointed. "Right there."

I spun to see the location of my greatest desire. A frown spread over my face. "Culbertson's? That's a department store."

My love's eyes gleamed. "Think of all the things they'll have. Sheets. Bedding."

"Um, there are bound to be other people there. Certain firsts might be best done in private."

"It'll be a first for me too, you know."

Here, a twinge of sadness took me. *How can that be true?*

Stormi continued. "That's where we'll register. You and I. A full day of shopping together."

"So, shopping." I exhaled. "That's the enjoyable part?"

"What were you thinking?" She walked by me, elbowing me hard in the gut.

I grinned and watched her for a moment, before gaining momentum and following her across the street.

I do not know how long we were in that store.

My mind fogged over after ten minutes of towels and bedding and kitchenware. I only know we emerged to a sun low in the sky, with a sheet listing items to be purchased for the wedding of Stormi Pickering and Jonah Everett III.

"You know, Jonah, there are some things we really should talk about." She swung my arm and we strolled down Main Street. We took a left at the library and wandered into Harmony Park. She and I plunked into the swings, and rocked gently.

"Things like what?"

"Well, let's start with kids. Yes or no, and how many?"

"Seriously?"

She shot me such a doleful look; there'd be no ducking the question.

"Okay, yeah, well, I like kids, in general. It would just be hard to see a bent-over little person and think, I did that. I caused that. And I'd hate to pass on my *Floppicus on the flooricus* to a kid."

She slowly nodded. "You won't."

"Won't have kids or won't pass it on?"

"Depends on how you answer my question."

I puffed out air. "Okay, well, we should have kids. I mean, as long as they're girls and look like you. It would be a shame not to."

"I agree," she said, settled. "But they'd be boys. And I want at least three."

"Three? I can hardly take care of myself."

"Which brings us to another issue. How are you going to make a living? I don't want to work outside the home when our boys come." She paused. "That museum isn't exactly gainful employment."

"Right." I considered the alternatives. "Maybe I take a job at the DairyWhip?"

"Think bigger, for us."

"Bigger. Like an I-could-do-anything type of bigger?" I stopped my swing and felt a swell. "If there was nothing in my way, I'd go to art school. It'd take forever, but I could maybe be a photographer, though that's a tough way to earn money. For that, I'd be a pediatrician. There are enough idiots working with kids; there should be one decent one."

My, how Stormi beamed. "Yes. That will do. Dr. Everett, with photography as a side hobby." She swung higher, repeating that name, and with each repeating the idea fixed itself firmer in my mind.

Yeah, I'll be a doctor. I could do that. I could do that well.

Stormi scraped her feet against the pebbles, slowing her swing to a stop. "Lastly, religion. Do you have a feeling about that?"

"I don't think we need to nail that down yet. My folks still haven't."

"We do, because I need to know what *you* believe, not your parents. I'm not going to get into arguments in front of the kids."

I let my mouth gape to remind her there were, as of this time, no kids.

"Well, I think there is a God."

"Agreed."

"I think the Catholic versus Lutheran versus Baptist stuff is all kind of silly, though. I always wondered why Gullary divides three ways down the middle every Sunday morning. So I'm not sure about the denomination question."

"Good answer, so far we're right on. What about the Jesus question?"

"Jesus question."

"Yeah, do you believe in a God who floats around watching us like ants in an ant farm, or do you believe really personal? Do you believe in a Jesus who gets involved in the affairs of men?"

Once again, I slowed to a stop. "If he's watching us, it would be a pretty pathetic show. I hope he's involved, somehow."

"He is." Stormi loosened her shoe from her foot. "Totally, he is." She started to swing, higher, higher, and on a forward thrust she kicked, sending the shoe flying at least thirty feet.

"Beat that."

With pain, I bent over and untied my laces, but as I started swinging, my shoe was farthest from my mind. I was rehashing the Jesus question, and like my pediatrician dreams, the more I thought, the more fervent my opinion became. It was calcifying. By the time I reached full swing, I could have preached a sermon.

I shook the shoe forward an inch, shifted in the seat, and swooped down to outdistance my bride. I kicked, only to find my leg was too long for the maneuver. It wedged in the pebbly ground and my body lurched forward toward a mighty face plant. I recall thinking how much it would hurt, and then thinking that Jesus might have mercy on me, as he most certainly was involved in this event. But in the second between my thoughts and impact, Jesus left, and Old Rickety showed up.

I never felt the ground.

I awoke, my face on fire.

Stormi and I lay alone beneath a starry sky.

On the left was a bowl filled with water, and a wet towel streaked crimson. Stormi sat up slowly, peering down at me.

"Welcome back. I think I got the pebbles out. You ground them in there pretty deeply. There's a kind man in that blue house right there. He gave me all this." She glanced around the park. "Jonah, that was the strongest seizure I've seen. I was a little scared." She rested her head on my chest.

"I'm sorry for scaring you," I whispered. "And right after we solved all our problems."

Stormi scooted down and placed both elbows where her head had been. She lay smack on top of me. At any other moment, a thrill unspeakable would have taken me over, but not right after. Right after, rest was all I wanted.

"Well, I'm glad you came back to me. Though you did waste six hours of our day."

"Six hours?" I squeezed my eyes tight, and opened them slowly. The world still shifted slightly. "You wasted four hours shopping."

"Wasted? We need things, you know."

But the spell was broken. "Stormi, you don't need to keep pretending. I think I pretty much ruined the moment. It was fun dreaming though."

"It wasn't a dream. This day, this wasn't a dream. Wait for me, you'll see."

"Okay, Stormi." I closed my eyes again. "I'll wait."

When next I opened my eyes, strength had returned, and the morning sun splashed crimson across the horizon.

Stormi sat on the base of the slide, staring up at that sky.

"It's time, Jonah." She turned and forced a smile. "I wish you could have sat up with me last night, but it's too late now." She rose and walked over to where I sat and held out her hand. I took it, and we walked back to the truck.

On the windshield, a white slip was tucked beneath the wipers.

"Great," I said. "When did the police come by? I'll get our ticket."

Stormi nodded and started the engine. I snatched the citation, turned it over, reading the small letters scribbled in a writing that was faintly familiar.

Time to go to work, Stormi. Grandpa.

I stuffed it in my pocket, and joined Stormi in the truck.

CHAPTER 17

Less than a week.

We'd been gone a matter of days, but as we pulled into Gullary, there was no feeling of coming home, or even returning to the familiar. The trailer homes hadn't changed, SMX still stood, nestled in hills and fronted by enormous chat piles, and the Welcome to Gullary sign still boasted of the 1980 boys' basketball trip to state. Visually, it hadn't changed.

But it was not the Gullary I knew.

I grew angrier with each turn, a bubbly rage that felt like betrayal. There were secrets in Gullary. And I had spent all my time in the museum unwittingly guarding them, silencing a man who lost his daughter. Perpetuating a red door policy that killed my sister. I'd been used.

"How do we do this?" I asked.

"Tonight we'll settle in, I suppose. Tell your parents you're okay. Tomorrow, I start."

"You mean we."

Stormi slowed in front of my trailer, parking on the street. "No. I'm going to need you, but not to help me. I'm going to need you free to move. I think things will get quite restrictive for me soon."

I didn't know what she was talking about. "So, what exactly are you going to do? Take out an ad in the *Gazette*? How do you bring up what's been buried for so long?"

"You'll see in the morning." She nodded toward the door. "You should get out."

Strange. Stormi spoke with certainty again; our run-in with Tres brought back the confidence that had always marked her. I, though, felt no need to obey. This journey ended where it began, but I wouldn't.

I slowly stepped onto the street. I turned to close the door, and then paused. "You know something more than I do. Did Tres tell you something when I was . . . out?"

"Exodus 20:5. Jonah, I love you."

"I, uh, love you too."

Stormi pulled forward, taking the left toward Greasy Jake's. I listened to the engine quiet in the distance, and set my face toward my old home.

"Okay, Dad, here we go."

I strode to the door, threw it open, and stepped inside.

The trailer was still, still and foul. Small details like dead sisters and dead seniors no longer hid. All was in the light, and the place felt evil.

No one had waited up for my return. There was no candle-light vigil. What had I expected? Not sure, but the pit in my gut made clear that I did not receive it. And then I did.

The world erupted with motherly affection. Hugs and kisses, punctuated by tears and how-dare-I's, then more hugs and kisses. Half of her seemed thrilled to see me, while the other half was near ready to end my life for her worry.

Finally, the tempest stopped, and Ma rubbed her eyes with the heels of her hands. "So, aren't you going speak? You could explain where you been."

"Of course he will." Dad walked out from the back, a forced smile on his face. "Of course he will. I'm glad you're safe, more than you know, but things are set in motion here. Things you do not know."

"Hmm. Things I don't know."

I walked by him toward my bedroom. His fingers clamped around my forearm, but I yanked free.

"Let go," I said. Inside, the rage returned. I had no more filter. What rumbled fearsome inside spewed out. I hated him. For what he did to Tres. For what I did to Tres. I thought in that instant to tell him all I knew, but I kept silent, for Stormi. She had asked me too.

Dad folded his arms. "It seems my concern was unfounded, Ma. Our son is all grown up. He feels no need to include us in his life. How wise he has become." He walked slowly around me. "And to think I tried to protect him, defend him, but you already knew that, right?" He fisted the neckline of my shirt and drew me nearer.

Ma took a step. "Our son is home—"

Dad's other hand shot up. "Our son left. Whether he returned, well, that's yet to be seen." He slowly released me. Strange, throughout the transformation of my father, I felt no fear. In fact, he struck me as small.

Flattening my shirt, Dad continued. "Three questions is all I have, and you will answer them. Where did you go? Who were you with? Why did you come back?"

I glanced at Mom, who covered her mouth with a shaking hand. She shook her head, ever so slightly.

"Well, Dad, the truth is I got married."

Mom gasped, but Dad latched on to the only piece of my announcement that interested him.

"So you were with Stormi."

I shrugged. "It's less romantic when your spouse doesn't attend the ceremony. Yeah, I was with her. I reckon your invitation will arrive tomorrow."

"Anyone else?"

My thoughts bounced off Arthur and Tres, Michael Queene and Winston. Maybe time would soften this moment. Maybe there would be a right time to share, but not yet.

"Anyone else?" he thundered.

"Nobody you care about."

I backed toward my room, feeling my way down the hall with both hands, freezing at the entryway to the kitchen. On the table sat Ma's Bible.

I quick-stepped over to it and dug through the table of contents. I fumbled through the pages, as Ma and Dad stepped into the room. There it was, what I was searching for: Exodus 20:5.

"Please, Jonah. You can talk to us." Ma stepped forward. "What's gotten in to you?"

I read the verse twice, and then lifted my head. I stared from Ma to Dad, before reaching for Ma's marker and ringing the verse in crimson red:

For I, the Lord your God, am a jealous God, punishing the children for the sin of the parents.

My eyes stopped there. "Guess that covers it," I whispered.

I spun and disappeared into my room, shutting the door behind me. I would spend the rest of the evening sitting on my bed, staring out my bedroom window, hoping to see some shadow of Stormi behind her shades. But I did not. It crossed my mind that perhaps she did run after all. Perhaps she dropped me off and fled. It would be the cruelest of moves, but I'd heard of wives doing worse.

A tapping at my window.

I couldn't tell which side of consciousness called to me, though I guessed it to be the tail end of the strangest dream. In the darkness, Old Rickety had come to call, and I was in the thralls. Yet I was enjoying it, in the same way I imagined a kid loved a vomit-inducing roller coaster, though I'd never experienced one. Round and round spun the world, and I heaved and rocked.

Faster. Faster.

Somehow, I could speak. Somehow I wanted more. More intensity. More, just more.

Is that all you've got, Ricky?

Then I was taunting that seizure. Even laughing at him. He didn't take kindly to my lack of respect, and he hurled me through my unconscious. But the tapping, distinct and clear, pierced the muddled voice of Old Rick, and I awoke sitting up, staring at that window.

I rose without difficulty and walked toward the face that beckoned to me. Stormi.

"Come," she said.

I followed, as if it were the most natural of things to squeeze out of my window at 4 a.m.

Stormi spoke quickly, her breath heavy as we marched toward SMX.

"What did you tell your dad?"

"That we were married."

Stormi broke out laughing, loud enough and long enough that I felt a pang in my chest. Then she kissed my neck, and the pang vanished. "Brilliant. Mention Tres?"

I was stuck on *brilliant*. It wasn't a word I'd experienced before. "Who? Oh, Tres? No. I thought I was supposed to leave that to you. Wait, where were you last night? I looked."

"Where were you looking?"

"Through your window." She slowed and raised her eyebrows. "I mean, I glanced periodically in the general direction of your window, you know, to make sure you were fine. I wasn't peeking or snooping or anything."

She sighed, and slowed further. "I was at the shop all night. Jake keeps all his old school stuff there. I needed this."

Stormi had been carrying an oversized book throughout our walk, but only here did I notice it. She handed the year-book to me, opening to a dog-eared page. "I needed the names of those kids who died. Sure enough, according to the juniors listed the year before, there would have been eighteen in Gullary during Lanie's senior year. Ten boys, eight girls. Here they are."

My eyes first fell on Lanie, raven black hair and a face a bit like Stormi's. She was beautiful. "I've seen them, well, especially her. In the Hive. I told you, Saul was blood-letting in front of her. These photos are all in the Hive."

Part of me had been holding out, casting a hopeful line back to Granddad, wondering if in the crazy world of killers and prophets, somehow my innocent family was sucked in by mistake. But the yearbook sealed it, and I kicked at the stupid ground with my stupid Everett foot.

"I was named after a murderer."

"A lot of people are." Stormi closed the book and we turned the last corner to SMX. "Jonah, I brought you here because I want you to see what I did. I want you to see exactly what I did. Because I don't think they'll be here long, and then rumors will start and I, I want you to know I did it."

"Yeah. Okay."

My gaze followed Stormi's outstretched arm. Up, up, to the top of the two chat piles. In the light of the SMX yard bulb, eighteen crosses shone white against the lightening sky. Eight on one pile. Ten on the other.

"Tres said that's where they buried them. Quick. Beneath a mound nobody would ever move. I put their names on each one. I marked them all. I did it."

"You did." I wrapped my arm around her and we stood in silence, staring up at our undoing, at the act that would indeed set things in motion.

"We never said our vows," Stormi said softly.

"No, we didn't. But if we had, I would've meant them, and I would have kept them."

She pressed into my side and wrapped her arms around my middle. "I, Stormi, do solemnly swear to . . . Aw, forget that. Jonah Everett III." She turned to me and took hold of my hands. "You have me. All of me now. No matter what happens. You have me now. The only me that's worth having. The me that nobody else has ever had."

I knew it to be fact, and I didn't reckon she could promise me anything more. A life together? That wouldn't be more. Growing old together? She couldn't give me that either. But she could give me her now. Standing in front of two chat piles and before the remains of eighteen witnesses. She could give me that.

I took a deep breath. She was waiting for words, hoping, it was clear.

"Stormi, I'll wait for you."

I hoped it was enough. In truth, the sentence confused me each time I'd said it. Outside of her request, why would I need to wait? But she said I should, and I reckoned I should firm it in a vow.

Stormi leaped into my arms, and though my back screamed, my heart soared.

"I'll hold you to it," she whispered.

Slowly, she released me, and she pulled me away from the mounds.

"What now?" I asked.

Stormi shrugged. "Now's the big pause. We alone in this world know what I did. It's peaceful, isn't it?"

It was. Words amplified. Every moment was clearer, more distinct. Every second mattered.

"But what if nobody bothers to look up there?"

"Oh, they will." Stormi leaned into me and took my hand. "Can I stay with you the rest of the morning? I don't really want to bump into Connor just yet."

I didn't answer. Of course she could, though the where of it was unclear. Eventually, I led her silently back to my door. My room would be safe for our final hours. We quietly entered.

Dad stood in the foyer, coffee mug in hand, tongue planted firmly in cheek. "Been out all night." He took a sip. "Good to see you, Stormi."

Stormi squeezed my hand. "Mr. Everett."

"You've been gone for a time. How was your trip?"

"Informative."

Dad's hard face softened. There was a part of him that loved the competition, reveled in the talk. You don't rise to power without deriving a bit of twisted joy in crushing a worthy opponent. He never found his equal in this home, but Stormi was a handful, and he knew it.

"Informative," Dad repeated, gesturing us toward the kitchen table, where the Bible no longer rested. "Inform me."

Stormi didn't follow, and Dad turned, the hard returning to his face. Yeah, he loved the game, but he hated when he couldn't set the rules.

"I'm going to spend my last morning with Jonah. We're married, you know."

"So I've been told, though I admit the news takes on a little more gravity coming from you."

Stormi released my hand. "You don't know who you have in Jonah. But that's okay, because I do."

He set down his mug. "I know my boy inside and out."

It felt like there might be a fistfight, and I pulled her quickly into my room. "What are you doing? Are you trying to make him blow? Wait, you are, aren't you?"

She smiled, though tired covered her face. "Angry people make mistakes. The chess game isn't over, and pieces will move quickly once the sun rises. I need to be sure your dad is one of them."

I didn't completely understand, and the two of us lay down on the bed and held each other. I felt no urge for more. I only wanted to fast-forward a year or two, in hopes that we could skip whatever happened next.

Next came swiftly.

The door swung open and Dad and Mr. Cartwright pounded into the room, grabbing each of us by the arm and pulling us toward the door. No words were said, but I knew where we were heading.

CHAPTER 18

The chat piles.

We stood silently at the base, while Mr. Gurney slipped and stumbled about the top. He was a good choice. Mr. Gurney wandered homeless through Gullary. Unattached and widely considered mentally challenged in any number of ways, Gurney was rumored to have served our country well in Vietnam. This, and general human dignity, earned him a place at most any dinner table in Gullary. But when Gurney spoke, the man was ignored.

He caught sight of us and slowed. Three crosses lay across his arms, and he was fumbling with a fourth. After an unsuccessful tug, he straightened.

"Hey Jonah, Stormi! Say, Mayor, there's names on 'em. Why are there names on 'em?"

Dad shook me. "Be clear, Jonah. Is this your doing?"

"Yeah, it is."

"No," Stormi said sharply. "It isn't. It was my doing. The crosses were my idea. The inscriptions, well, they're Gullary's doing, but you already know that. Jonah knew nothing until this morning."

"I told you about her. Now you understand the threat." Mr. Cartwright hauled Stormi in front of Dad. "She buried my Gina, and now she's trying to raise—"

"Who?" Stormi called out, firm and strong. "Say your child's name. Who's under there? Doesn't it eat at you, Mr. Cartwright? Don't you wake up and go to sleep under a cloud? How about you, Mr. Everett?" She glanced at Dad, and peered into the sky. "I'm not blaming, I'm just saying. I bet losing a child destroys a man."

Dad's face changed a sickly shade of white and he looked to me. He knew that I knew about Evangeline.

Color returned, and Dad lowered his head. Slowly, he reached out and pried Cartwright's fingers from Stormi's arm. He was evil, but not cruel.

"Stormi," he spoke slowly, "you realize you waded into some things here that are before your time. Have you spoken with Tres lately?"

Here she smiled, soft and settled. "I've spoken with my grandpa."

Cartwright pushed her aside, and shook his head. He took hold of Dad's shoulders, but Dad's gears were spinning, his eyes fixed on the ground.

"Girl's lyin'. That ain't possible," Cartwright spoke. "Tres's lost girl was only eighteen. She had no child."

Dad's hands shook. "Tres had an older daughter. He did. She left here and Stormi could be hers." He cupped hands around his mouth. "Gurney! Get a move on!"

Gurney worked with speed, stumbling across the second chat ridge. He no longer gathered up the crosses, but rather pitched them down on the far side of the pile. On the ground, Dad's worry sent Cartwright into a frenzy. He paced back and forth, muttering as if his mind had soured.

I was watching the failure of Stormi's plan. A news ad would have been much more certain. There were better ways to spread word through a town.

Stormi eased toward me and winked, nodding toward the distance.

In the midst of all the confusion, a wind had picked up, swirling dust around the chat pile base. When the wind cleared, young Leonard, Kyle, and Colton, each eight years of curious, peered up at Gurney with gloves swinging from bike handlebars.

"What you doin', Mr. Gurney? Ain't you supposed to stay clear of them piles?" Leonard called.

Gurney froze, the words that fell from his lips doing more damage than any news ad could have done. "Hey, Leonard. I'm not rightly sure. Mr. Everett and Mr. Cartwright told me to dig the crosses out of the chat, and that's what I'm doing."

Secrets take a long time to construct and strengthen. It only takes two sentences to shatter them. Those boys shrugged, and then biked toward Gullary's ballfield, but Colton reached down and picked up two crosses on the way.

Dad and Cartwright took off after him, but Colton knew the rules; if an adult is in pursuit, you must possess something of value and you do not stop.

Mr. Gurney had a bird's-eye view of the whole affair, and glanced down at Stormi and me. "Do I keep on going?"

"No, sir," I shouted. "Leave those last two up there."

Gurney slid down. "Glad of that. Creepy business. And what of these other crosses on the ground here? Over ten of 'm."

"Did you recognize any of the names?" Stormi asked gently.

"Last names. Most folk in town."

Stormi took a deep breath. "Maybe deliver them for me, if it's not too much trouble."

Gurney started to pick them up. "Glad to, Stormi. Glad you're back. Gullary was mighty boring without you." He mouthed the name on the cross at his feet, bent over, and reached it to me. "Here you go. Easy enough. Evangeline Everett."

We watched him shuffle away, his arms filled with the past.

I clutched the cross in my hands.

"I'm sorry, Jonah. I really am." Stormi raked her fingers through her hair.

"You should leave here now," I begged. "Cartwright lost his head, but he'll come back. Dad too."

"They will. I'll be waiting right here." Stormi kissed me. "But you should go. I'll need you before this is done."

I glanced into the sky. Clouds had rolled in. "You know that for sure? Because I don't really want to leave you."

"You won't." Stormi pushed me away. "You promised."

I don't know which was more effective: three kids peddling Gurney's testimony, or the hand-delivered crosses. I suspect they worked in tandem. But the result was a scene I had not witnessed before.

My vantage point was the DairyWhip, filled with memories of Arthur. From an inside table, I watched the older residents of Gullary scurry into town, then vanish across the street into Orton's Drug. Folks went in. Dad and Ma went in. Three cones later, they had not emerged.

An hour passed, and Cartwright hopped from his truck, Stormi in tow. Again, he hauled her beneath the shoulder, though he needn't have done so. For her part, she looked at peace.

Why Orton's Drug, I did not know. There was nothing to distinguish the business from Gullary's other few establishments, other than its designation as Gullary's oldest. Once Orton's Drug Emporium, and before that Orton's Mercantile, Orton's had been a fixture in this part of Oklahoma for generations.

I rose and crossed the street. Though the store sign had been flipped to read *Sorry, We're Closed*, I slipped in. Mr. Orton was not seated behind the counter, nor was Roger, his mutt hound, usually wandering the aisles. Backroom voices raised, and I eased down the painting supply aisle toward the storeroom. The door was ajar and I ducked beneath the tarp rolls and peeked inside.

Women wept. Men wept. I thought I'd encountered every type of cry in Gullary, but those were normal cries. These reminded me of Saul's from the Hive. They were not of this earth.

"Quiet, all!" Dad said. "None of us thought we'd ever need to make use of the meeting place."

"But then, none of us knew that an unnatural would fly in!" Cartwright.

"But we all knew we had a hand in killing our babies."

For a moment, the weeping stopped; all sound, really. "You know it's true. I'll say now what we all know, but were too afraid to say then." I had never heard Ms. P silence a room.

"Martha's right. We did this. We allowed it. This falls on us, not Stormi."

Ma?

"There's nothing to revisit. We've worked through it. We survived." Mr. Cartwright took the floor. "The question at hand is what we do now. Our misfortune is barely contained. Leonard and Kyle especially are unconvinced. Now, they're but kids, but Gurney, the old coot, he's talking all over town."

"What is he saying?" Stormi's voice sounded peaceful, and I breathed deep.

Cartwright cleared his throat. "You've said enough."

"No, the question is valid." Ms. Utica, the English teacher, spoke up. "I'll tell you what he's saying, because he told me. He's saying that you and the mayor asked him to climb up on a toxic pile and remove a bunch of crosses, and that each cross bears the last name of someone from this town. Why treat Stormi like a criminal? Where's her part?"

I always liked Ms. Utica.

"Why are you here?" Dad asked. "You don't have anyone who . . ."

"Who what?" my teacher pressed.

And just like that, Ms. Utica was shoved from the room, and the door slammed.

"Look around! Make sure only the kids' families and those involved are here!" Cartwright boomed, and I stood. Ms. Utica grimaced and straightened her blouse.

"Something's afoot, Jonah. I followed the herd, and something's afoot."

"Two somethings, probably."

I stared at the wall, and the idea that my Stormi was trapped on the other side sickened me. I stayed because she asked me to, but it was all I could do to remain. On the wrong side of the door, a door I suddenly noticed had been painted red.

CHAPTER 19

Stormi was right.

The message spread.

With Ms. Utica, one of the few articulate people in town, asking questions, there was no way Dad could hide what had happened. He was a quick thinker, but he wasn't Houdini. I left Orton's and slowly walked down Main, turning onto C Street. The few nice homes in town stretched out before me, including the red brick beauty on the left. Arthur' house.

I took a deep breath, slowly climbed the steps, and rang the bell.

Arthur answered, but did not raise his gaze to meet mine.

"I was wondering when you would stop by. We went through an adventure. Wouldn't you say it was an adventure? Normally, people who go through adventures become friends. I thought that before our illegal adventure we might already have been friends. Certainly after, though."

I had no words. Death had been quick to take people of late, and I didn't reckon it planned on giving any back. But there Arthur stood, and then I was hugging him. He stiffened, not hugging me back.

I released him and stared and frowned and stared some more.

"Why didn't you tell me? You idiot! Do you know what I've been going through? I came here to tell your dad—"

His face lightened. "You thought I was caught up in the fire." He smiled broadly. "I wasn't." Arthur paused so long, I almost hit him. "I should have been. Absolutely, I should have been. But the gas keeper, number nineteen if you are referring to him by number . . . Isn't that strange that they used numbers? I think if I chose a number for myself, it would be twenty-eight, after my birthday, but it was probably taken, and then there would be two of me—"

"Arthur!"

"The gas keeper came running out right after I gave you the can, before I went in for more, and I couldn't go in then and I hid. Actually, I dropped onto the ground, but I'm quite flat and—"

"Arthur."

"He dashed into their prayer shack and came out with a candle, hurrying back to his cabin. He must have needed the flame to see, but gas and candles don't sit well together. Do you know about the laws of combustibility?"

I reached out, covered his mouth, then slowly uncovered it.

"He wasn't in there ten seconds before the explosion occurred. You were gone when I reached the garage. I thought you left me." He paused. "Why did you leave me?"

I opened my mouth. I had an answer, but it sounded flimsy and weak. Why does anyone leave anyone?

"It was my fault. I shouldn't have."

"So, I started walking. I walked twelve hours, and the next evening, I hitched back to Gullary. I thought I'd find you."

I nodded. "Yeah. We, uh, took a day off."

"A day off? I don't understand."

"It doesn't matter. Like I said, I came to tell your dad that you're dead." I placed my hand on his shoulder. "Glad you're not."

I turned to leave.

"Hang on. Do you want to come in? There are some strange events happening."

I'd never before been inside Arthur's house, a solid build with a wide foundation and a crawl space. It struck me how much I did want to stay here. Facing my parents felt hideous. Heading back to work at SMX even more so.

"Yeah, I'll hang out for a while."

I wish I could recall all of Arthur's room. The space miniatures and children's toys positioned on shelving units, the disassembled computer equipment strewn everywhere; this my mind still holds. But the knock downstairs came so forcefully, Dad's voice sounded so unsettling, that it filled all my brain's remaining memory.

"Jim, Margaret, the town's holding a gathering tonight at Jake's. We need you there."

The heat that night was overpowering. Not that we were strangers to sweat, but every few weeks an evening arrived with a vengeance that emptied streets and drove us into bought air.

But there was no space in Gullary large enough to fit the town. The Baptist church came close, but I wondered if a sanctuary meeting hit a nerve with Cartwright. Instead, an outdoor meeting was planned inside Greasy Jake's fenced yard. Three hundred plus heeded the call and filed into the dusty world where Stormi once lived

Seating proved tricky, the few decent chairs Jake owned reserved for the oldest and frailest among us. The rest grabbed tires and hubcaps and fenders, and plopped down. I stood against the fence, waiting for Stormi.

She didn't come.

Nor did anyone else of the young variety, and none that were in the Villa were wheeled in either. The few new families were also absent. This was a meeting of those who held power, and of this group, not a single head could I find missing.

Except Stormi.

Dad grabbed a wrench and pounded on a fender. Jake winced at the clang.

"Thank you for coming. We needed to speak to you all. Given the unfortunate events of this day, the Circle thought that perhaps you ought be aware of facts, so you can discern for yourself what is true and what is hearsay."

"Tell me why my neighbor had a cross planted in his yard!"

Bless Ms. Carlisle. The woman had no filter. A murmur went up, as many, especially on the outskirts, had their first encounter with today's activities.

"What cross?" Mr. Ingersoll, a hard-working farmer/hermit who we only saw every few months, folded meaty arms. He undoubtedly was inconvenienced by the meeting.

Dad raised his hands to no avail, and resorted again to the wrench.

"I'll get straight to it. Stormi Pickering, a girl we all know to be a bit—"

"Unnatural." Cartwright finished the sentence.

"By cloak of night, she planted crosses in our chat piles. If her confession is true, and I for one believe it, she needed a high-profile area to make her point." Dad shot me a glance. "I know a lot of you are close to Stormi. You've come to love her over the years she's been with us. I understand the sentiment. I'm still driving my Chrysler because of the care she put into it." He turned to Ms. Utica. "She sat in your classes, ate with your children, grew up in your homes."

At this, Ms. P. began a slow shake of the head. Connor sat still as stone beside her.

I wanted him dead.

"But Stormi, as you know, was never one of us. This, the extended culmination of her last school project, proves the point."

Dad was joined by the other members of the Circle. An ominous group of men, I might add. Cartwright stepped to the fore.

"Seems Stormi was taken with the plight of the Cherokee in Oklahoma. A worthy concern, to be sure, but one abnormally urged on by a book read right before school's end in literature class—ain't that right, Ms. Utica?"

Ms. Utica opened her mouth, but no words came out.

"*Hear My Flight*—wasn't that a book assigned in your class? Did not discussions about injustice follow? Was Stormi not most vocal in her outrage?"

Ms. Utica nodded, defeated.

"Well, it seems that Stormi felt obliged to do more than talk. The crosses on those chat piles, in your yards, based on a confession from her own lips, were meant to make you realize what it felt like for Cherokee families to lose their children. The names pulled from an old yearbook, like the one Jake reported missing not hours ago. Isn't that right, Jake?"

Jake was tortured. His face said it. "Missing, yeah, but she worked for me. She was privy to all I owned—"

"It was a cruel act by her, to be sure," Dad interrupted, "but one urged on by one of our community's most trusted teachers."

More murmurs. Ms. Utica hung her head, and Dad's gaze found me. *Do not speak, son.* I read it perfectly. *Do not speak.*

I watched as Dad's words took root, deepened in the fertile soil of a desperate town. I felt the Circle's hold tighten, deepen. *I'll need you before this is all over.*

"That's a good story." I winced, my back screaming as I stepped into the ring. "A good story, Dad. Is there any more to it?" I stared at Ma. "Is there a chapter about Evangeline? Do you remember her? I don't. I don't remember my sister. I never got to meet my sister. I was never told about my sister."

Dad took a step toward me. "Enough, Jonah!"

"It's been long enough, all right. Today, by the chat piles, I finally saw her burial cross."

Ma's knees buckled and she toppled, caught on the way down by Ms. P. I turned slowly.

"Do any of you remember Lanie? She was beautiful. I've seen pictures. Daughter of Tres Cantor. She died the same night as my sister. There are sixteen more stories where those came from. Eighteen kids from this town are dead and buried beneath those mounds." I pointed at the piles in the distance. "Eight girls, ten guys, teens like me. Teens like me and Stormi. Let's tell their stories now!"

"That true?" Mr. Ingersoll asked. "That where they all went? There was no accident?"

Ms. Lowell burst into tears. "I can't. I do not care what happens to me, to us. I can't. It's true. Every word Jonah spoke is true. My Patricia, she's under there."

I did not stay to hear the rest, but hurried toward the gate as hundreds stood, confused and hollering.

I glanced over my shoulder, catching Dad's eyes, filled with both hatred and another emotion I scarcely recognized: admiration.

"Where is Stormi? We've got two stories, and I for one need to hear her intent!" Mr. Ingersoll's voice cut through the mayhem.

Where is Stormi? A sinking feeling struck me. *Where is Stormi?*

Oh, Lord.

I said my first real prayer.

CHAPTER 20

I lumbered home, snatched my gallery keys from the nail in my room, and hopped on my bike. Shouts in the distance made it clear the meeting had not ended, and I tore toward SMX in solitude.

I pulled past the guard tower, and a gust caught me. A loner. On a still night, from nowhere, a renegade wind nearly toppled the bike. It was gone as quickly as it had come.

"The Herald," I whispered.

Just legend, of course. But we'd seen enough tornadoes in our day to compile quite a body of twister lore. Some folks in town swore they could feel twisters coming in their bones, others looked to their pets for warning over the Tulsa weatherman.

We all treated our superstitions with a twinkle, knowing they were suspect at best. But not the Herald.

A wind born of nothing and heading nowhere. An orphan ghost too strong for the moment. I looked up. Not a cloud. Yet this only cemented the fear in my gut. A Herald had arrived.

A storm was coming.

I doubled my speed, dismounted while still coasting, and threw down my bike against the gallery door. A minute later, I was inside. Ten seconds more, I was in a familiar well-lit hall.

"Stormi? You here?"

"I am." She sounded frail, dispossessed.

"That you, Jonah? Your voice is a sound for these ears." An arm stuck out of the cell. Gurney continued. "What they done this for? Ain't done nothing but for 'm."

I jogged toward Stormi, sitting on the floor in Tres's old cell. Gurney was in the terror hold next on.

"Right back, I can get you out," I said.

"No." Stormi held up a hand.

"Yes!" Gurney kicked the bar. "Girl's gone loco in her brief confinement."

"Think, Jonah. If you let us out, you become a part of this. I told them you know nothing. I told them you were seizing while Tres told me what was done. They won't bother you. Right now, you can move freely."

"No, I don't think I can. See, a town meeting turned south. Dad and Cartwright shaded you as an activist on some activist cause. Not a bad cause really; in fact, it was doggone believable. So . . ."

"You spoke up."

"I spoke up."

"In front of the entire town."

I rubbed my forehead, wincing. "Pretty much."

"Pretty much?" Stormi broke into a wide smile. "Should I make your bed in here, or wait until they arrive? Jonah. You've changed." She reached out her hand. I grasped it. Yep. If there had been any doubt, it no longer lingered. I was messed up in love.

"Don't mean to interrupt, but it seems I could be let go without doing much additional harm. I didn't even know what I was doing."

"That's good, Mr. Gurney." Stormi stuck her lips out the bars. I wanted them, but let them move. "You not knowing was a good thing, but my guess is this might be the safest place for us to be. Jonah knows we're here. It'll take some time for them to figure out what to do with us. We'll wait it out, until maybe the storm dies down."

The storm.

"Stormi. I felt it on the way in. The Herald."

She stepped back, and then took her place near me. "Strong?"

"Almost took my bike."

"Sky?"

"Clear."

She rubbed her hands, and I could see her thinking. "Listen, it's coming. You need to get your dad to admit to what's been done. The truth needs to be said. The Herald didn't find you by accident. Gullary is out of chances, unless your dad— unless the *Circle*—confesses to what they did."

"How do I get him to do that? After tonight, he's not going to turn a listening ear."

Stormi stroked my cheek. "You are brave. You are changed. You'll figure it out. I've done my part, now finish it."

"You want *me* to finish it?"

Stormi gazed at me with eyes filled with pride. "Tres got this one thing wrong. He was waiting on me, when all this time you were the strong one. It's always been you."

I felt a smile sneak across my face. I would finish it. Me. *Floppicus bendicus*. It felt right. According to Tres, Stormi blew in to condemn this town, but now standing free on the outside, I reckoned she had a different purpose all along. She didn't come to change Gullary. She came to change me.

I straightened. "I guess I best head home. Dad is going to want to talk, I suppose."

"You sure I can't be of assistance?" My, Gurney looked pitiful. "Out there?"

"Sorry, Mr. Gurney. I'm sorry you were caught up in this. I'll be back to check on the both of you."

I left the way I came, pushing aside the doorstop and letting the door click behind me. It sounded so final, and in truth, I wasn't certain I would be able to return.

Still, the Herald chose me. I had no choice.

"You came back."

How dark our living room was.

How emotionless my dad's words.

I quietly shut the front door. Dad's outline sat black against the opened, moonlit window. He didn't turn to address me.

"Where else was I gonna go? This is home."

His shoulders rose and fell.

"It was a brave statement you made, there, in front of everybody. I give you that. Took some doing for me to get matters back under control."

"How could you lie?"

"How could I not?" Dad turned, and though his features were barely visible, he struck me as smaller, less imposing. "There are so many things you don't know."

I slowly sat down across from him. He was first to wade into the extended silence.

"I loved him, you know, your grandpa. Idolized him in every way, and there was reason to. Things were rough here. It wasn't safe for families. His family. Your family. It was his job to curb the violence poverty brings." Dad shook his head, continued speaking into the night. "He had the idea of using the prison in a secondary fashion. What was I to say? I was young. So you can be as mad as you want about whatever you're angry about. Cause as much trouble as you want for me, but that anger is all misplaced."

"But you knew about what happened. You said nothing."

Dad paused. "I don't know what you expected me to do. The system was in place. It worked. It had never failed. And then it did and it took my daughter and broke me, but I had a responsibility to protect the people of this town. I can't expect you to understand responsibility. You're like your mother that way, thinking with your heart instead of your brain."

I started to rise, pushed up halfway.

"Wait."

I eased back to a sit, and he continued. "You're sensitive, Jonah. But you're not as uninvolved as you think. Your back. Your seizures. I always reckoned those ailments were sent to smite me. A curse for what'd been done on your grandpa's watch, left undone on mine."

"My seizures aren't a curse. They just are."

"Yeah," Dad whispered. "But how I hated them, maybe you. I thought they were about me, and for that I'm sorry, Jonah. You deserved better."

The chain around my gut loosened. Dad had apologized. I couldn't remember hearing such from him before. Maybe there was hope, hope that the Herald could be silenced. "Why can't you apologize to everybody now? Like you did to me."

"Follow the thread if word gets out. The local press. Soon national news, son. We would be the story, and what would happen to us, Jonah? What would happen to our family? To other families living on grief? They would take good parents away from their children over wrongs committed twenty years ago. They would destroy more families. No, we can't go back."

Something like fog settled in that room, as Dad's logic took hold. I tried to find the right and the wrong, but they were muddled, lost in years and hurt.

"But Tres said the storm that took SMX, he said that was a judgment. He said the bus accident that took Gina was another one, stopped by Stormi. If that's true, I don't think you can run from this. Dad, I felt the Herald."

Dad shifted. "When?"

"Tonight. You were at Jake's. You know there was no wind. Not a trace."

A crack opened in Dad. I felt his wavering.

"Jonah, I'm not speaking about that superstition. When did you speak with Tres?"

"I brought him food forever; we talked then. A little more when he found Stormi and me, but that has nothing to do with what you need to do right now."

"I was under the impression that you were out of mind by the time he tracked you down." Dad hesitated. "At least that's what Stormi said. You contradict that story?"

The door opened and Cartwright filled the frame. I glanced back to Dad. The crack was filled.

"Yes. I mean no. Old Rick came right after Tres did, and when I came to, Tres was gone. I still don't know all he said to her."

Dad leaned forward. "Own up, son. Isn't it true that you knew all about the SMX incident before you left to find Stormi? You've long been planning to take out your anger on me." His voice sounded strained. "You and Stormi have been waiting for a chance."

"Don't turn this!" I softened. "When I left . . . When I left, you were my hero."

"I'm sorry, but sentiment aside, the boy is clearly part of the scheme." Cartwright stepped forward. "Partners with Tres from the start. He knows everything, and as long as he shows determined to fill the air with Tres's lies, for the greater good, he needs to be held. Come with me, Jonah."

"What lie am I telling?" I glanced at Dad, who fiddled with his lip. "Dad. Please."

His body slumped. "Do it quickly, Cartwright."

"No sir, let's take our time here awhile."

Our gazes spun toward the door, toward Tres. He looked large, imposing. Safe. "How you doin', kid?" Tres pushed right by Cartwright and strode to my chair.

"Honestly, I'm not sure. I think my dad is about to throw me in jail, and Stormi's already there, but aside from that, we're great."

"You did good, kid. Stormi did good." He turned to my Dad, now standing. "Do you really want to add to your legacy by pitchin' your own son into a cell? Why now? Because he knows a truth you need to speak?"

Silence.

"Nothin' to say to me? You have me in a prison for years without cause, and you feel no urge to make comment?"

"Tres, it wasn't that easy, and you know it."

"Oh, you're right on that. Let me tell you exactly how hard it was. Sitting in a cell while my daughter screamed not three feet away. Can you imagine hearing that?" Tres turned. "Can you imagine that, Mr. Cartwright?"

Cartwright slumped heavy into the wall, I imagine tilted by the weight of guilt.

"Do you want to know what Evangeline shrieked? Do you want to hear her words?"

"Please, no," Dad whispered.

"How about you, Cartwright? Care to hear what happened to Alan, what he said? Listen."

What Dad and Cartwright heard in the next minutes, I do not know. I myself heard nothing. But from the way they tore at their ears—the way Dad slumped from his chair—I reckon it was the stuff of nightmares. A child's last moments. Chilling.

"Now, the men who done that?" Tres continued. "I have three with me outside. For all we know, they was the ones to take my own girl from this earth. They's still payin' for the crime. Still in their cells, if you ask me." Tres's presence filled that dark room. "All I want, Mr. Everett, is for you to come clean on what's been done. Follow me out that door. Do it for the one you loved."

"Get out," Dad seethed, his breath heavy.

"This is your last opportunity, Mr. Everett."

"Get out!" Dad threw himself toward Tres, landing far short and on his knees, where he clawed at the carpet. I'd never seen Dad cry, and I admit that in that moment I wanted to throw myself beside him, grab hold of him, and rock him. I wanted to tell him everything was going to be all right. But I knew it wasn't.

"Come on, Jonah. I know what you said upon arrival, but this ain't no longer your home."

I rose on instinct and followed Tres away from everything I'd known. I didn't know the destination, but I knew the words were true. That wasn't my home. My home was with Stormi.

"So, now we get Stormi, right?"

"Now we wait. We see what your dad does. Gullary's last chance."

"Last chance?"

We stood across the street for five minutes. I glanced at the trailer, the town, Tres's face. The strength he'd shown was gone, and in his eyes was a sadness I'd never before witnessed. Tres became the old drifter. Without strength. Without anger.

Without hope.

He hung his head. "I just came from seeing Stormi. She told me the Herald's been sent. Time's up."

"And you left her in there?" I glanced around town, expecting to see some horror slowly advancing through our streets, but my gaze snagged on a small clump of men coming my way. They walked slowly, deliberately, three undertakers moving shoulder to shoulder in the middle of the street.

"These guys again? You brought them?"

"I brought them."

They reached us, and we stood awkward in the silence. One placed a hand on my back, but the thought of what that hand may have done years ago made me sick, and I jerked away.

"Jonah," the tall one said soberly.

"How did you three . . . What about Michael Queene? You got away again? Why come back?"

He cleared his throat. "There's living and there's living with yourself, and they aren't the same thing. In the Hive, we've been doing the first, but the second has proven elusive. Being back here, well, knowing perhaps there's a good part for us to play in this story, it's worth the risk."

"Part to play? What part?" The thought of Evangeline floated through my mind, tried to form, take shape. I could almost see her laughing—hear her telling me I was her favorite brother—and then she was gone, like so much vapor. "You've done enough here. Taken enough."

The tall one winced, as if struck. "It's a truth we live with. More confining than prison ever was. But maybe we can help others find their way out."

He glanced over his shoulder. A row of minivans and pick-ups snaked slowly along Main Street, their beds stacked high with boxes and picture frames, bicycles and small children. Lots of children. Seemed half the population was heading north out of town, but not just the young ones. Ms. Utica's yellow Jeep, Dr. Only-Doctor-in-Gullary's white Toyota Corolla—even Gurney's rusted moped tooled on by. Behind the main procession rolled a bus from the Villa, half filled.

"What's going on?"

Tres gave the tall undertaker's shoulder a squeeze and faced me. "Gullary's Exodus. Lot of innocents in this town. A lot of folks have clean hands and knew nothing of what was done. I brought my own heralds to give warning."

I couldn't break free from the straggling vehicles departing. Greasy Jake's roadster, Ms. P's station wagon . . .

Ms. P?

I grabbed Tres' arm.

"Ms. P's getting out? She knew! She knew everything about the red door and probably about Connor and what he was trying to do to Stormi and . . . why'd you tell her?"

Tres pried loose my fingers and patted my cheek as though I was a little child. "Mercy, Jonah. Even in this, look for it. We warned everybody." He forced a smile and tousled my hair. "Got a safe place you can go? You can come with us; we won't go far."

"For how long?"

"Until."

I thought a moment. Stormi was still here.

"I can't leave her."

Tres rolled his eyes. "She's not your concern anymore. Never was. Her purposes here are done." He leaned in. "Let. Her. Go."

I stared at this man, and started to laugh. I do not know where the joy came from, or why it came. Maybe nerves, but I wasn't anxious. Laughter bubbled up in waves and splashed out of me and over me and maybe I was going crazy, but in that moment I knew exactly my trajectory, and Tres, who knew everything, was clueless.

Finish this.

Wait for me.

"No."

Tres frowned. "No, what?"

"No, I'm not leaving her. As long as she is here, I'll be here. Easy as that."

"Do you have any idea what you're doing, boy?"

"None whatsoever!" And the cluelessness of love felt positively buoyant. "Don't worry, Tres. There's Arthur. I didn't see them leave. I could stay with him, I think, depending on his parents."

"So, the boy lived. That's good," Tres said. "Hard to find a suitable opponent these days." He smacked my back. It did not hurt. "So your choice is made. Okay. You find your way to Arthur's on your own?"

"I've lived here all my life. Gullary is my home."

"Good-bye, Jonah."

He gazed long at me, a remembering gaze of the uncomfortable kind. The kind you give when you are trying to make a memory.

The four of them walked toward a van parked across the street.

"Tres!" I rubbed my head. "I'm not going to see you again, am I?"

He leaned against the tailgate, mosquitoes buzzing him beneath the streetlight. "There's a little of Stormi in you, huh? You tell that girl I'm proud of her. Kiss my grandbaby . . . kiss Nayeli for me."

The van pulled out of town, and I watched it go.

Stormi. Nayeli.

I turned, knowing my job was to wait. I would give Dad three days to speak, and then I would find a way to finish it.

I didn't get three days.

For two hours, I wandered through an unnatural calm. The streets were deserted, and even the dogs and chickens held their breath. I alone moved in Gullary, a town once a movie, but now trapped in a still photo. Only the crunch of sneakers on gravel hinted that I was alive, that any of this was real.

Not a whisper of wind. Maybe I didn't feel the Herald after all—

The lost breeze heard my thoughts, and swept back into Gullary the moment my foot landed on A Street. By B Street, his brother had arrived, stiff and steady. But it was not until C Street, when Papa Gust showed up, that I felt fear.

Winds are not equal. Living in Oklahoma provides ample opportunity to study airflow. Winds blow straight, and winds spiral. They updraft and press a body down, like so much gravity. But they also carry emotion. Light and breezy, well, that's joy. Firm and forceful, there's a relentless strength to it, and it makes you say uncle. Oklahoma also is home to flirtatious, peek-a-boo winds, disappearing and reappearing with a wink and a nod.

And then there was the wind that hit on C Street. It came hard and fast and angry. There was a rage with it, no, *in* it. It was looking for something. Looking to do something. Something horrid. I ran to Arthur's buffeted by that wind. It grew in power so that I did not think of the hour upon arrival; I simply pounded the door.

The siren wail took care of the rest.

Arthur's dad threw open the screen. He fumbled with a robe and his glasses and the situation simultaneously, flattening down his hair and blinking hard.

"What?"

In that instant, my needs changed. Yeah, I had to find shelter, but Arthur's crawl space would not do.

"We need to go. Siren's up!"

"Gissy! Arthur! Grab and come!" His mind clicked on, and the words came rehearsed and urgent.

I turned toward the street, suddenly alive with motion. People scurried toward the underground community shelter, toward security.

Stormi.

I bolted toward SMX beneath the warning's throbbing wail. It cut through the gusts, but only slightly. When the siren sounded distant, Gullary knew, a storm was nearly upon us.

I fought forward, and at times sideways, but minutes later I reached the gallery. The front door banged open, and I raised my arms to protect my head and burst inside. Light on. Brick lodged against the red door.

Stormi slept.

I threw open her cell door with a clang. Stormi stretched and rolled over, sat up peacefully on her bed. The roof creaked. The roof of the impenetrable Supermax prison creaked.

"We need to go! There are sirens."

"You lead." Stormi stood and took my hand, and my heartbeat slowed. We would be okay. The storm would pass. We would be together.

After all, we were married.

We walked into the gallery, and pushed outside. Rain fell horizontal, and puddles raced across the prison yard.

We broke into a run, toward the shelter.

"I need to head home." Stormi's voice barely reached me. "I need something!"

"No time!" I tried to yank her, but she slipped free. "Bad idea! Really bad!" We veered down a street filled with rolling garbage cans and airborne tree branches, and slipped into Stormi's trailer. She disappeared into her bedroom.

The winds howled, and outside, metal and wood crashed against trailer walls.

"Hurry up, Stormi!" I ducked in after and froze.

Connor knelt on top of her. Groping in the storm.

Stormi fought, her screams swallowed up by the wind, and rage took me. I blinked and suddenly there were two Connors and two Stormis. The pre-seizure aura muddled my senses. I had little time. I lunged toward the nearest Connor, and felt my palms grasp solid neck, and then all feeling vanished, leaving only sound. The sound of wind and the screaming of children. My mind left this earth, as Old Rickety joined the storm and had his way with me.

But Old Rick must've known a big storm when he saw one. He didn't want to stick around either.

He departed as quickly as he had arrived. Uncharacteristic. And with his exit, my faculties returned, and I again felt skin. Connor's skin. I saw my hands still grasping his neck, and his body, limp on the ground.

"No." I released him and felt for a heartbeat, listened for breath. I found both, and fell back against Stormi's desk.

"He needs help. We need to tell someone what I did. I'm not covering this up, I'd be no better than Dad."

A tree limb crashed through the window, and Stormi hauled me to my feet. "Nobody will believe you, they'll think it was me." She tore at her dresser, grabbed a photo, and slid it into the back pocket of her jean shorts. "Okay! We need to get to the shelter."

"But we can't leave him!"

The front door flew open and crashed through the trailer, which rocked and settled.

"Now!" Stormi's voice was terrible.

I stumbled up and we pushed outside, arms crooked before our faces. A minute later, the leaves fell still. In that moment, silence. The world was unnatural.

"It's come," Stormi whispered, and I heard her. "Run!"

The roar surrounded. It was no train. It was alive, a creature, twisted and bent, come to gather up everything to itself. Hell was here. Stormi and I reached the shelter and dropped to our knees, pounding on the metal door to the underground bunker. It cracked, and then faces called to us from the dark. I descended, glanced up. Stormi was not following.

"Nope! Not today, Stormi!" I shouted. Hands grasped me from behind, but I broke free and joined Stormi back outside.

"Wait for me!" she called. "Please, wait for me to come home."

She kissed my neck, and around us the wind seemed to calm and the rain sprinkled a gentle note. I grabbed her with all I had. I kissed her, full and strong, searching for more. Stormi's eyes opened wide and then closed and for a time we were together. Completely. I lifted her from the earth and spun her, one with the winds around us. We would not leave one another. Ever.

Then she pushed hard, broke free and stumbled away. She ran into hell.

"Nayeli!" I dove to catch her, but grasped nothing, as the leftover seizure took me yet again. When next I came to, I huddled with all of Gullary in the dungeon, while the tornado raged overhead. Ma's hand gripped mine, but I knew the truth. I was alone.

CHAPTER 21

It's a strange thing, the workings of wind. What it takes, what it leaves, what it changes along the way.

As I sit on my step and gaze, I see little of what I knew. Gullary is gone, wiped clean, as it were. The chat piles, and I reckon those laying beneath, sucked back into the sky where they belong. Two years have passed since SMX was again reduced to foundation, though already talk in nearby towns has shifted to the importance of rebuilding the prison, a testament to pride, and to how hard it is for lessons to be learned.

Yep, Gullary is wiped clean. Except for one set of steps. Ours. And one bedroom. Mine. My photos were untouched, and those waiting to be hung rested undisturbed on my desk throughout the storm. Memories of her I treasure.

It is strange what the wind leaves. And though I've no illusions that my room will be spared future storms, it makes me feel good that it's lasted this long. Now, looking back, I'm also relieved that Connor was found pinned, but mostly whole, beneath his front door. Had he not survived, my weekly pilgrimages back to this place would have carried an entirely different feel.

Things taken? Seems Old Rick was a casualty. I've had not one hint of a seizure in the twenty-four months since the leveling.

The citizens, also. I've heard no eagerness to resurrect Gullary. Still, the familiar is tough to abandon, and most families migrated a mere seven miles or so to Waxton, with the balance moving deeper into the palm of the Ozarks, to the other side of Lake Gullary. The cement cauldron that remains marks what we once thought ours, and holds the sum of our lives in broken glass, brick, and cloth. Maybe my undertaking to write the record of what transpired will end up buried as well. I can't shake the feeling that I was central to the story for a reason, to record what killed this town, just as the truth was meant to give it one last chance.

Which brings me to Stormi. Of the living, she alone was swept away, though I believe this now to be her plan all along. In the months following the storm, I lost myself in the reporting of nearby towns, hoping for a breeze of news. What goes up generally does come down. Though I am not certain the laws of physics hold true for Stormi. I will, however, hold fast to her final words, and I will wait.

Foolish, my dad says, though he says little else. He wanders through his days a broken man. Ma waits for him to return, as I wait for Stormi.

Waiting, it gives purpose to time. Stormi said that once, so I will keep coming back, and someday, I will see her again.

I place my pen down as a cloud passes over the sun. Just one cloud, tiny and round, the only one in the sky. I stare at that cloud until it shifts and the heat of noon blazes once more. I think to add the cloud to my account and lower my gaze.

"Hello, Jonah."

Both of Me

Jonathan Friesen

It was supposed to be just another flight, another escape into a foreign place where she could forget her past, forget her attachments. Until Clara found herself seated next to an alluring boy named Elias Phinn—a boy who seems to know secrets she has barely been able to admit to herself for years.

When her carry-on bag is accidentally switched with Elias's identical pack, Clara uses the luggage tag to track down her things. At that address she discovers there is not one Elias Phinn, but two: the odd, paranoid, artistic, and often angry Elias she met on the plane, who lives in an imaginary world of his own making called Salem; and the kind, sweet, and soon irresistible Elias who greets her at the door, and who has no recollection of ever meeting Clara at all. As she learns of Elias's dissociative identity disorder, and finds herself quickly entangled in both of Elias's lives, Clara makes a decision that could change all of them forever. She is going to find out what the Salem Elias knows about her past, and how, even if it means playing along with his otherworldly quest. And she is going to find a way to keep the gentle Elias she's beginning to love from ever disappearing again.

Available in stores and online!

BLINK

Aquifer

Jonathan Friesen

Only He Can Bring What They Need to Survive.

In the year 2250, water is scarce, and those who control it control everything. Sixteen-year-old Luca has struggled with this truth, and what it means, his entire life. As the son of the Deliverer, he will one day have to descend to the underground Aquifer each year and negotiate with the reportedly ratlike miners who harvest the world's fresh water. But he has learned the true control rests with the Council aboveground, a group that has people following without hesitation, and which has forbidden all emotion and art in the name of keeping the peace. And this Council has broken his father's spirit, while also forcing Luca to hide every feeling that rules his heart.

But when Luca's father goes missing, everything shifts. Luca is forced underground, and discovers secrets, lies, and mysteries that cause him to reevaluate who he is and the world he serves. Together with his friends and a very alluring girl, Luca seeks to free his people and the Rats from the Council's control. But Luca's mission is not without struggle and loss, as his desire to uncover the truth could have greater consequences than he ever imagined.

Available in stores and online!

BLINK

Connect with Jonathan Friesen!

www.jonathanfriesen.com

 /AuthorJonathanFriesen

 @FriesenJonathan

 /friesenbooks